Seven Steps to Heaven

First published by Jacana Media (Pty) Ltd in 2007
Second, third, fourth and fifth impression 2015
Sixth impression 2016

10 Orange Street
Sunnyside
Auckland Park 2092
South Africa
+2711 628 3200

© Fred Khumalo, 2007

All rights reserved.

ISBN 978-1-77009-387-4

Cover design by publicide
Set in Sabon 11/14pt
Printed and bound by Mega Digital (Pty) Ltd, Cape Town
Job No. 002653

See a complete list of Jacana titles at www.jacana.co.za

Seven Steps to Heaven

Fred Khumalo

One
Words Are Swords

The cockroach crawled across the table top, pausing every now and then to probe the air with its antennae. It looked lonely, lost. It was famished. As fate would have it, it stumbled upon a pool of human vomit at the extreme edge of the table. This pungent mixture of yesterday's half-cooked ox liver, gobs of porridge and God-knows-what-else was swimming in a sea of cheap wine. It presented itself as an interesting proposition to the wandering cockroach, which immediately got down to business, eating voraciously. Now and then it raised its horns to the heavens as if in gratitude to the gods of Cockroach Land for providing such a feast.

As the cockroach continued with its excited exploration of the numerous islets of vomit, it stumbled upon what felt like a human hand. Startled, it shook its horns disapprovingly before it scurried away. It disappeared into a crevice underneath the table.

The hand which the cockroach had touched belonged to one Sizwe Dube who, in his unwitting benevolence, had provided the cockroach with its morning feast.

Sizwe was sleeping in a foetal position on top of the table. He was fully clothed in a nondescript suit of dark colour. His snores came out in long, tortured rumbles. Now and then he would stop snoring and start chewing some invisible morsel of food. There was a sling of vomit at one corner of his mouth. Even in his sleep, he still held in his left hand a half-finished bottle of cheap gut-corroding wine known in township parlance as Ngigoduse Nkosi – Take me home, O Lord. In his other hand he held a cellphone.

The table on which he was sleeping stood in the middle of a huge room illuminated by a gas lamp hanging from the ceiling.

Slivers of pale natural light entered the room through the slightly parted curtain hanging from a window. Outside, the skyline had assumed a purplish hue, marking the beginning of a new day.

The room was barely furnished. In addition to the table, and lining the wall, were four beer crates that evidently served as seats whenever it became necessary. The walls were garishly adorned with a menagerie of posters featuring liquor advertising, half-naked black models, soccer stars, famous musicians – and the flavour of the century, Nelson Mandela, in various poses. Alongside one of the walls stood a sagging couch on which sat two young men. Unlike Sizwe, they were not asleep. They were sharing a zol of marijuana. They smiled now and then, patting each other on the back. The boys sported the bloodshot eyes of people who had not slept for a number of days, or people who had been smoking too much marijuana, or people who had had too much to drink. They were whispering something to each other. One of the boys nodded his head in the general direction of the figure slumped on the table. The other responded by shaking his head furiously in disapproval, pointing his finger towards an adjoining door.

The boy with a deep black face and a trace of moustache took one last drag on the zol. He threw his head back and exhaled a white tendril of smoke into the stuffy air. He smiled with satisfaction and threw the remains of the zol onto the linoleum floor. There the discarded joint joined the other remains of yesterday's life: stubs of cigarette, empty beer bottles, half-finished bottles of wine, morsels of food, and a used condom.

He got up and took two tentative steps towards the table at the centre of the room...

The adjoining door suddenly flew open. The boy froze in his tracks, his eyes popping out as if hypnotised by the figure framing the open door.

A hulking giant of a woman in a nightie so short and transparent you could see the dark mound at the joining of her thighs stood with her hands about her waist.

'For the sake of Zachariah the Zulu,' she screeched, 'y'all rats are still here! Every rat to his hole, right now! Voetsek! Go go go home!'

She started waddling her big frame towards the boys, but then paused when her eyes landed on the figure positioned on top of the table. 'Modimo!' she cried in a squeaky voice that belied her huge size, 'y'all have guts to vomit and sleep on my imbuia table?'

'Sis Joy,' the dark boy stuttered, 'it's only poor Bra Sizwe. Prob'ly overdid it. But, hey, you know what he's been like of late. I don't know what society does to our writers.'

Joy the shebeen queen took a deep sigh and shook her head like one in deep despair. 'That sounds like very civilised talk coming from you, you bloody thug. I'm surprised that you even know the existence of the word society. The way you go about, I am sometimes convinced that you were not born of a human being but some monster from hell, the way you go about stabbing people for their own money!'

'Aw, Sis Joy, it's people like you who make me forget about turning a new leaf. I haven't been on the streets for the past two weeks, trying to get my life back in order, but Sis Joy is insulting me again as if I haven't tried to be a good boy.'

Sis Joy gave the two young men a malevolent look, and said, 'I have no time to talk about morality and society to you. Just fuck the hell out of here.'

'But, Sis Joy,' the dark boy said pleadingly, 'can we have just a half-jack of Oude Meester? You know, a teeny-weeny bit of old Mpandlana.' He produced a crisp hundred-rand note.

'Just this once, and you leave.' Sis Joy's face softened as she snatched the note from the boy's hand. She crinkled her nose and said, 'Kort Boy, I wonder who has died. I sure hope to Mvelinqangi, the god of the Zulus, that this is not blood money.' She glared at him, turned on her heels and disappeared into another room.

A few minutes later she returned with a half-full bottle of Oude Meester. She plonked it onto the floor in front of the two boys.

'You dirty rascals,' she said when she realised that the boys were gaping at her, their eyes peeling the flimsy clothing from her plump body, 'I'm old enough to be your granny. What are you doing undressing me with your eyes?'

The boys looked away, their Adam's apples dancing guiltily.

She clapped her hands firmly, saying, 'Y'all drink up like men now. Quick-quick! Y'all have to leave my place so's I can clean up for new customers. You've had your turn at my trough, give room for other thirsty pigs to indulge!'

'Okay, Sis Joy,' the quiet boy said taking a huge gulp from his drink.

Sizwe, the man lying on top of the table, punctuated the end of the verbal exchange with a loud fart. 'Sies!' Joy cried disgustedly, and whipped the curtain open, suddenly flooding the room with light. She opened the windows, allowing the morning breeze to come in and chase the bad odours out.

But even these adjustments could not rid the room of its smells that clung stubbornly onto the walls and the pieces of furniture scattered around. The room smelled of human sweat; of stale farts and stale beer; of marijuana; of sex; of sin; of vomit; of unfulfilled dreams; of broken promises; of violence. But that was to be expected. The room served as a shebeen. It was called Joy's Oasis, located on the roof of Hillbrow Heights, one of the busiest blocks of flats in the inner city slum of Hillbrow, Johannesburg. It was a place where men like Sizwe drowned their sorrows. Problem was that booze didn't drown these sorrows; it only made them float to the surface. It was a place where people like Sizwe hoped to meet and share the camaraderie of kindred spirits caught in the endless debauchery called human existence. It was a place where the Sizwes looked for violence that they hoped would end their miserable lives. It was an oasis that never slaked any thirst, it only dehydrated the sons of long-suffering mothers, husbands of sex-starved wives.

No sooner had Joy left the room than the dark boy took a cautious step towards the figure on top of the table. One step. Pause. Two steps. Pause. Three steps. Pause. Look around. Clench fists. Don't mind the beads of sweat on the upper lip. One more step, look around... yeah, getting there, getting there, baby...

Kort Boy finally reached the figure on the table and touched the hand holding the cellphone. With just one prod, the hand gave and the cellphone was ready to be dislodged from the limp grip...

But then the cellphone started ringing loudly.

Sizwe sprang into life, his fingers closing around the cellphone. He spoke gruffly: 'What-what!? Sizwe, the most famous journalist in the country here, start talking.'

Groggily, he got down from the table and slowly straightened up. Sizwe was a tall, dark man with an angular face. His head was clean-shaven. He had a proud forehead, hollow cheeks. The whites of his eyes were almost brown, the result of continuous hard drinking. The pupils were pitch black. He could outstare the devil, people in the streets said. A knife scar ran from his left temple across his cheek, down to his chin, a typical facial design for a man who walked, drank, fought, made love and cried on the mean streets of Johannesburg.

As soon as his eyes opened, a phrase rang in his mind: 'When I was young, if I made soup...' But the phrase lingered in his mind, unfinished.

He started tottering about the room. He kept saying to the phone, 'Ja, I hear you... I hear you... what? Ja, I follow... but what do you think I am? A fucking computer, press a button and the book writes itself? I know I've missed my deadline several times, but this is a difficult story to tell. I am suffering, man. I know you're supposed to be God himself, fucking editor that you are. But hey, I'm doing my best. You know a lot has happened to me recently... I've lost so many loved ones... what? You don't give a fuck what's happened to me? Tell you what. I'll write you a cheque right away, return the advance money you've given to me if that pleases you, you fucking bitch.'

He threw his cellphone into a corner, screaming like a wounded animal.

'Words kill because they are swords,' Sizwe was mumbling to himself, walking about the room. 'Words. Sword. Words are lethal. Words are dangerous. They betray us to the world in which we move. You open your mouth, and you've bared your soul to the world, to fucking stupid editors who just won't understand. You've exposed your essence, your spirit to the world in which you move. Words are ideas. They are molecules of one's soul. Piled on each other, one after the other, words formulate a body of thought, a body of belief. But these philistines won't believe me when I say I am stuck. The book isn't happening as planned. Sometimes I think I am one of three people; sometimes I think I am Thulani, or Thulani lives in me... sometimes I think I am the third one... I think.'

The door to the adjoining room opened again, and Sis Joy appeared. Her bulk was framing the door. She was smoking a joint.

Sizwe wiped his mouth with the back of his hand and cleared his throat, and addressed Sis Joy. 'Madame, shit, I don't know,' he said, tottering slightly. 'My ma, hoor my, I fucking don't know.'

'Stop talking in parables, jou moer, what's cooking?' she said.

'Shit, I don't know.'

She gave him a look that said 'Don't give me that crap again; I'm not giving you another loan' but she said instead, 'Haven't you started working on the book again? Why are you losing your focus? Why are you wasting your life away when you've got so much talent?'

There was hurt in her voice, and tenderness. Sizwe could only grunt, 'Fok, you old magreezer. What do you know about words on paper, about books? Who do you think I am? Just watch this space.'

His knees buckled and he fell down, breaking the bottle of wine he was still holding in his hand. He started sobbing. Sis Joy went to the corner where the music system was situated. She fiddled with the knob, and the morning suddenly exploded with the sound of Harold Melvin's 'Wake Up Everybody'.

She went back to Sizwe, who was now lying sprawled on the floor. She kicked him hard in the ribs, screeching, 'I said you can't go on like this. Wake the fokking up. Where are your balls, man! Don't be a fokking moffie. Stand up and be proud like a real manne, you donner se jelly-kneed moffie. Go and finish the job that you started. You've been talking about this book you've been paid to finish writing, yet every time I see you here you are drunk out of your skull. Talking all the incomprehensible shit about firing squads. And while you are busy writing that bladdy book, go have your head read as well. You are a good man, God knows that, but you've become a coward. You're losing the plot!'

Groaning, Sizwe pushed to his feet and made ready to leave.

The two boys had meantime collapsed onto the sofa. Too drunk, wallowing in a heavy haze of marijuana. However, at the sound of Sis Joy's screeching voice – 'Voetsek! I said gerrup!' – they were startled out of their stupor, got up in a hurry and left.

Walking slowly towards the door, Sizwe kept saying, 'Fok, you old magreezer. This here Zulu boy will show you what he's made of.'

Sis Joy took his arm and whispered, 'I'm sorry, my sweetheart. Got carried away there, mkhulu. But you have to collect yourself. I can see your publisher is putting you under pressure.'

'The bitch is bugging me.'

'But there's more to it than meets the eye. There's something else bugging you. What is it?'

Two

Baptism of Fire

After leaving Sis Joy's Oasis, Sizwe ducked into a café and bought himself a litre of cold Coke. He threw it thirstily down his gullet to fight the moerse babalaas that was making his head throb painfully. He was kinda sober now, but his head still ached terribly. He smelled like a combination of a brewery and a garbage dump. His suit, once glamorous, was shiny with grime and had the unmistakable look of having been slept in more than once in the past few days. It was still speckled with vomit.

Sis Joy had at least allowed him to brush his teeth and wash his face in her bathroom. Nevertheless, his eyelids still looked droopy, his lips dry and chapped. His whole face was ashen.

Walking down Pretorius Street, he checked his watch. Eight a.m. It was a Saturday. The streets were already abuzz with people. There were noisy hawkers plying their various trades on the crowded pavements. Cars were blaring their horns. Taxis weaved through the busy morning traffic, trying to get to their destinations as fast as they could.

His mind was lucid again. He started thinking about the conversation he'd had with his publisher not so long ago. The conversation invariably got him thinking about events of the past month when he'd gone to Zimbabwe. To witness a childhood friend of his facing the firing squad. This thought itself flung him back into the past.

***

The first time they'd met, the sun was stingy with its warmth, peering from behind a mass of dark clouds. It wasn't exactly cold.

It never was cold in Durban, not even in winter. But it wasn't hot either. Both boys had felt obliged to wear jerseys, long pants and sneakers. They were about nine years of age, both of them. The street was deserted, except for the two of them walking towards each other.

'Yes!' the boy with the yellow complexion and curly hair said in what he hoped would pass for a greeting. But to the other boy it sounded like a challenge, as if it meant, 'This street is mine, what are you doing here?'

'Yes!' the other boy responded in what he hoped was an equally challenging tone. He was ready for any eventuality.

'You're new here,' the yellow boy said, but to the other boy it sounded like yet another challenge, an accusation.

'Yes, who isn't new?' he said, picking up the gauntlet. 'You are new as well. These houses are new.' He was waving his hands around at the neat rows of houses on either side of the road. They were neat, tiny, and visibly new, in pastel colours of dirty pink, yellow, cream, with tile roofs. Each house stood proudly on its piece of ground, each plot separated from neighbouring plots by a shiny fence. Each piece of ground itself looked new. There was not a tree in sight, not a blade of grass, not even a piece of paper. The streets themselves were new. Each street was a dark black ribbon fringed by dull grey pavements. The smell of fresh tar still hung strongly in the air. The street lights were tall, majestic, shiny and new. It was just too perfect, like a page from a kiddie's picture book. Where lawns, and verdant flower gardens and rockeries, and shrubs would have been were blankets of pink sand, as if the new houses had sprouted from under this blanket of new granules.

The two boys stood glaring at each other, each of them waiting to see who was going to look away first. The yellow boy cleared his throat noisily. Then he spat into the face of the other boy. He waited for a response. And got it. The other boy cleared his throat noisily, dredging spit from the depth of his body. He spat into the yellow face. They glared at each other, hands balling into angry fists. Then they turned and walked in opposite directions.

They had each taken about five steps when they turned almost simultaneously, each looking across his shoulder. The yellow boy said, 'I'm not scared of you, monkey face.'

'Who's scared of pumpkin face, yellow-as-shit face?'

Two weeks later, the two boys bumped into each other again. The yellow boy was carrying a two-litre bottle. He was walking briskly from the shops. The other boy was heading towards him. As the distance between them narrowed, the dark boy's nostrils were attacked by the tangy smell of paraffin.

'Ah,' the dark boy said in mock surprise, 'I see your parents are oh-so-like-yesterday. They are still using paraffin to cook their food when the rest of the neighbourhood is using electricity!'

The yellow boy was dumbstruck, then fired his own salvo: 'Monkey face, give me all the money you have – now!'

'Or else?'

'I'm warning you. Give me your money now!'

Before he could repeat 'or else', the black boy saw his adversary taking a quick gulp from the bottle of paraffin. Just as quickly, the yellow boy spat it into his face, and flicked a matchstick.

Boom! The black boy's eyes were blinded by a ball of fire, and he could smell his own burning hair. Fire, fire...

Three

An Indecent Hour

The movie of his life as a boy continued to play in his mind's eye. Now he was remembering how he had spent a week at the local clinic, recovering from the slight burns he had suffered at the hands of Thulani.

In the meantime, his parents Mandla and Thoko had finally located the home of the culprit.

'This piece of shit needs to be sent to jail for what he's done!' Thoko, Sizwe's mother, cried to her husband as they prepared themselves for an encounter with the culprit's parents.

'But he's only a kid, my dear,' Mandla said. 'Calm down. The boy doesn't belong in jail. Let's handle this in the style of ubuntu, African civilisation.'

'Jesu Mariya Josefa! What are you talking about? My child, my only child, has almost been killed, almost burned to death like Satan's friends roasting in hell, and you come telling me calm down. I'll make you come down from your ivory tower of good manners and respectability and civility.'

She charged at her husband, ramming him in the pit of his stomach with her head. Caught off balance, Mandla howled in pain, staggering backwards until he hit the stove with his behind. The pots were knocked off the top. A spurt of gooey, boiling stew licked Mandla's face as he hit the floor with the back of his head. He was out cold.

***

Now, in spite of the facts, the crude reality that he had witnessed the executions first hand, Sizwe was finding it difficult to accept that Thulani, the man he'd known from so long ago, was the same person who had wound up being torn apart by the bullets of the firing squad in a foreign country. It had been a long journey indeed. He kept thinking of him as 'the man he'd known' instead of remembering him as a friend, the brother he'd never had. He, somehow, thought that by distancing himself from him, by denouncing his friendship before the harsh present realities, he would be spared the pain. The pain of losing his friend, the pain of actually witnessing the cruel manner in which he had been killed.

* * *

Another cinematic flash of memory: Now it is a week after his parents fought. His father has recovered from the burns he suffered when the stew fell on his face. But the parents still haven't visited the home of the culprit. His father is sitting on his chair, on the front porch, enjoying the sun this summer morning. He is watching the parade of people going about their business along the street.

Although still new, the suburb is now showing some vivacity, a spirit of communality gradually bringing the people together. Almost overnight, the yards are covered with fresh grass. This is thanks to government trucks that have been going around over the past few weeks, sprinkling white grains along the sides of the streets and onto people's yards. The stuff is actually seedlings for a new, fast-growing strain of grass.

Wattle trees have also been planted at regular intervals alongside the road. Seemingly it is hoped that when these trees reach their maturity they will form some kind of canopy protecting the streets, like the jacaranda trees that form colourful canopies over the streets in white suburbs.

In his back yard, against some vocal disapproval from neighbours, Mandla has built a huge enclosure from pieces of wire mesh and corrugated iron. The enclosure has been populated with about eighty ducks. In the middle of the enclosure is a pond with stagnant smelly water. The ducks are quacking and shitting, burdening the surrounding air with the stink of their droppings. Mandla learnt the art of rearing ducks as a young boy growing up in rural Underberg, where he was born and grew up before heading for the big city.

The ducks in his enclosure are not strictly for the household pot. He breeds them and sells them to neighbours to supplement his income from the shoe factory where he is employed as a sweeper. From the extra money he makes from the sale of animals he can afford to indulge in the simple pleasures of life, like enjoying a few bottles of beer now and then.

Incidentally, this being a bright Saturday morning, Mandla is sipping steadily from a jug of beer. He's sitting in his chair, legs spread wide apart, the better to create enough space for his belly which is hanging in front of him, jiggling this way and that, as if it has a mind of its own, whenever he coughs.

People are walking proudly up and down the streets, chests pushed forward in the manner of a person who is proud of his achievement: a house in a new, beautiful suburb. The suburb is called Exclusive Park. The houses here are not like the usual four-roomed matchboxes in the old townships that sprang up in the 1960s. After all, these are the 1980s. The black man in South Africa has moved on. He now lives in a house that he owns, not one he rents from the government. Okay, the government still has a hand somewhere because the company that finances most of the houses here is highly subsidised by government.

Most of the people here are government servants: teachers, policemen, nurses, clerks, the lot. The government is trying to prove a point, that those loyal to it will be appropriately rewarded; the anti-government radicals can rot in their tin and plastic shacks. This here is progress. Each house has electricity and running water and an inside toilet, unlike in the 1960s and 1970s when black people had to be content with using paraffin stoves, candles for illumination, and had to relieve themselves in night soil buckets. Of course, those who can't afford to pay for their electricity still use paraffin stoves and candles or paraffin lamps for light. But this is frowned upon here. You are letting the black folks down by bringing habits of the old townships to this new Exclusive Park.

People here get hurt when you call their neighbourhood a township. It's a suburb, they say, a suburb. Each house now has a neat lawn, and each house has been assigned a huge gate for the car, and a tiny garage. It is expected that all hard-working servants of government will have cars, if they are not already driving. Some of them have even built swimming pools at the back. They have removed the wire fence surrounding their yards, to replace it with concrete slabs that come in a variety of designs, turning the houses into mini-fortresses.

The owners of these fortresses are your merchants – butchers, shopkeepers, and keepers of shebeens, the popular drinking places. There is constant competition between the government employees, who boast about the smattering of education that they possess, and the merchants, who admit that they are not educated but are clever enough to have wrestled away from the clutches of the apartheid government to make themselves and their families comfortable. Keep your government jobs and your education to yourselves, they jeer, but we the merchants have the last laugh because we can afford to eat meat almost every day – which *you*, with all your education, can afford only once a month on your lousy salaries.

Mandla is still sipping his beer slowly, occasionally rubbing his tummy, belching loudly and nodding with satisfaction. Jesus, there's nothing like your first beer of the day! He has made up his mind that as soon as he's finished with his beer he will take a stroll to Paradise Road, a shebeen just a block away. He can hear the thud of the music coming from there already. It's only eleven thirty in the morning but he can sense from the sound of the music, and the number of people sauntering in the direction of this house of happiness, that if he doesn't move quickly he will miss out on a big party.

He has to move fast so he can join the boys for a couple of beers. But most importantly, he wants to be with Lovey, the shebeen keeper's daughter. He is in the process of taking a long swig from his beer when he is startled by his wife's voice.

'Mandla, husband of mine, father of my child!' says the wife in a not-cheerful tone. 'Why are you drinking beer so early in the morning? Don't you have the patience to wait for a decent hour before you start drinking?'

'Decent hour? This is beer, not a doctor's prescription. I can drink it any time, anywhere. The label on the bottle doesn't say "Drink at a decent hour", or does it? I am not the educated teacher, you are.'

She glares at him. He loves her even more when she flares her nostrils angrily, her whole body – otherwise slender and tall – suddenly growing in size like a startled bullfrog.

He looks at her face, angular with high cheekbones. Her complexion is unnaturally light, thanks to the fashionable skin-lightening creams she has been using to wage war against her blackness. What self-respecting black city-born girl didn't know the efficacy of these skin-lightening creams? Men scoffed at the idea of their wives using these creams: 'Aren't you proud of your blackness? You will never be white, no matter how many times a day you scrub your face, no matter how many wigs you have that look like a white woman's hair.' But behind the backs of their women, the men bragged to each other: 'But have you seen how light my wife is now? Not like yours, who looks as black as the devil. Buy her Super-Rose, man, or Ambi, so she can look like my own wife, who is now like a real coloured. Her cheeks look like sun-ripened peaches. Invest in Super-Rose or Ambi, but if you have to go really downmarket, console yourself and your wife with Memafoza. You won't regret it, sonny. Imagine playing with those cheeks that look like sun-ripened peaches. Oh, sonny, let's stop talking about this, I'm getting excited!'

The lighter the woman, the more catcalls she received as she walked down the street, married or not married.

In any case, it was befitting Thoko's class to use these skin-lightening creams. She was a city-born girl, highly educated, and came from a Christian background. These black Christians had internalised western values. Why, they spoke English among themselves even though Zulu was supposed to be their home language.

Thoko was a teacher at the local primary school. Neighbours, friends and members of Thoko's family couldn't understand why, with all her sophistication and all the education under her belt, she had decided to marry an uneducated farm boy who worked as a sweeper at a shoe factory. Not a manager, not a supervisor, not a salary clerk, not even a simple dispatch clerk, but a sweeper! Before she found him the job at the factory he had been working on the construction sites. He had been one of the labourers responsible for the construction of a number of townships around the city of Durban. Even back then on the construction sites he had not been a supervisor, not a dispatch clerk, not even a bricklayer, but a simple dagha boy – a person whose job it was to mix concrete and trundle it all over the building site in a wheelbarrow.

By the time they acquired a house of their own in this township they had been married for nine years, having tied the knot immediately after he impregnated her.

'You know,' neighbours and her relatives would whisper when Thoko was not around, 'we would forgive Thoko if Dube was a dish of a man, a well-dressed man-about-town. We would understand that her heart had been stolen by his handsomeness, that her eyes had been blinded by his sense of style. But his looks are nothing to write home about.'

'You are wrong there, my sister. You can write a whole book about his short squat legs, about his beer belly which reaches his destination before he has even embarked on his trip.'

'I wonder how they do it, you know what I mean, with such a big tummy which surely must get in the way.'

'But what about those yellow teeth of his.'

'She must have bought an extra large pillow to accommodate her husband's double-decker head.'

'You know, that head is so misshapen, I think he was dropped on it when he was a kid.'

'And we know all about people who were dropped on their heads as young children.' The speaker pointed obscenely at her temple, to indicate what she thought about their subject's mental state.

'Maybe that's what Thoko needs, a mentally unstable man she can manipulate and kick around.'

'But what about the children?'

'Are you surprised they only have one? Even he is an excuse for a child. He walks around like one in a dream. Twice, he's almost been knocked down by a car because he doesn't check before crossing the street, always absent-minded.'

'But my children tell me that Dube boy is the best in class. Speaks well too.'

'What do you expect? He doesn't expend his intellectual energies on ordinary things like other children. His escape from his sorry state is schoolbooks. I bet he knows all the arithmetic tables, and the names of all the capital cities of the world when they do geography...'

Four
Stop Irritating God

Meanwhile, oblivious to what was being said about them elsewhere on planet earth, the Dubes were glaring at each other, with the man still holding his half-finished beer and the wife standing in front of him, her hands on her waist.

'You know,' she spoke now, 'it's been almost two months since my boy was attacked by that criminal who wants to pass for a boy, but you have done nothing about it! Nothing!'

'Ah, mama kaSizwe, that's water under the bridge, my dear darling, my coconut cake. Sizwe has surely forgotten about it. Why scratch wounds that have healed? Why cause our boy unnecessary pain?'

'Unnecessary pain, huh? You know, every time Sizwe goes to the shops, I have to wonder if he'll come back in one piece.'

'Ha-ha-ha-ha!' he laughed, throwing his big double-decker head back, his tummy jiggling before him. 'You don't have to worry about his safety, I tell you. Sizwe can take care of himself. He can do a few karate chops, he can box, he can use stones, and most importantly, he's good with his sticks!'

'Sticks! I've been telling you for a long time now to stop forcing my boy to carry those sticks! I don't want my boy to grow into an uncivilised barbarian like you. I will make a doctor out of that boy, a lawyer.'

From the time he was six years old, Sizwe had been drilled in Zulu stick-fighting by his father. Father and son could be seen doing mock battles on their front lawn at some weekends. Passers-by would soon gather into a crowd, watching, admiring, sometimes laughing at the two.

'What do they think this is?' disgusted onlookers would sometimes scoff. 'This is Exclusive Park, not some godforsaken Zulu reserve. If they can't stand the ways of the city they must pack their smoke-smelling bags and fuck off back to the sticks.'

These were the comments that outraged and embarrassed Mrs Dube. After all, she was an upstanding citizen, a highly regarded teacher at the local school, but she had a tree bark for a husband, as an unrefined person was called. The bark of a tree.

'Okay,' he was saying now, draining his jug, 'what are you proposing now? How do we move forward?'

'How do we move forward? What a question! We put one foot in front of the other, and so on. Let's go to that boy's parents and express our displeasure. We must warn them that should their brat lay his paws on our child again, it's jail for him. I've got friends and colleagues whose husbands are policemen who are bored out of their skulls at the lack of criminal activity in this neighbourhood. They will be highly excited and grateful if I were to alert them to the criminal activities of that boy who attacked my poor boy.'

'Do you know who the boy's parents are?'

'I don't care. Let's go to their house now!'

Dube smiled, and said, almost to himself, 'Some people are always on the lookout for embarrassment.'

'I still have the address of the house written on a piece of paper somewhere in my handbag. Now let's go before it's too late.'

Sizwe, who'd been standing at the kitchen sink listening to the argument outside, thought of sneaking out of the house by the back door. But he was too late, for his mother came bustling to the kitchen, saying, 'Let's go to the house of that criminal.'

'What criminal?' He had to pretend he had not been listening.

'The criminal who burned you.'

'Aw, ma, but is it really necessary? That was a long time ago. Besides, the boy is no longer giving me trouble. I can take care of myself, as you know. We go to the same...'

'Hey, hey, you! I wasn't asking for your opinion. I said let's go! Don't be stubborn like your father!'

'But do you know who his parents are?'

'Hey, hey, you!' she said, boxing his right ear, 'I don't need to hear from you. Let's go!'

Dube's tummy emerged from the lounge, signalling his imminent arrival in the kitchen, where he intended rinsing his beer jug and disposing of the empty bottle of beer. Father and son exchanged amused glances, winked surreptitiously.

Almost in unison, they said to the woman, 'Okay, let's hit the road.'

***

Sizwe's mind switched back to the past again, to that moment when he and his parents were hastening up the street towards Thulani's home.

'This is the house here,' Sizwe said, pointing at what looked like a six-roomed house painted a bright apricot colour. There was a single garage on the side, with a yellow Toyota Corolla parked just outside. 'This is the house, Ma.'

'But,' she said, looking at house and looking at the address written on the piece of paper she had in her hand, 'but it can't be.'

'The boy said this is the house,' Dube remarked. 'What's the problem? Have you changed your mind?'

'But this is somebody else's house.'

Dube moved fast, opened the gate and walked across the lawn to the front door. The boy followed and, at a distance, the wife followed reluctantly. Confusion was written on her face.

On the third knock the door opened. There was a flicker of recognition as the woman who opened the door scanned the three faces.

'Oh, come in,' the woman of the house said, 'Madam Dube, Mr Dube, please come in.'

'Thank you, thank you,' Thoko Dube said as she walked in, followed by the son, and the husband coming in at last, bumping his big tummy against the door which the woman of the house was trying to close, thinking they were all inside. She was mistaken. Only Dube's tummy had succeeded in making it; the rest of him was still outside. Finally they were all in, and welcomed to take their seats.

'What have we done to warrant a visit by such respectable people as the Dubes?'

The Dubes exchanged furtive glances before the wife decided to break the embarrassing silence. 'Oh, my dear neighbour, it's these kids of ours that bring us together. They always bring us grown-ups together, don't they.'

'Aw,' the woman of house said, 'I thought you were teaching at junior primary, not at senior primary where my son Thulani is a pupil. Or have you changed schools? What has my son done now? He has always been naughty at school, I know.'

'My dear neighbour, it's got nothing to do with school.'

'Then what is it all about? Tell me it's got nothing with the political violence that is prancing about the land. Our suburb has been left untouched by this scourge, and may God keep it that way.'

Just then a tall lean man walked in. He wore black pants and a priest's dog collar. Now Mrs Dube's suspicions were confirmed. This was the house of her Anglican priest, Father Tembe. Although she went to church every Sunday, she had never seen the priest at close quarters, let alone exchanged a word with him or his wife.

Now the priest was smiling, greeting all of them and saying, 'Aw, my dear wife, I heard you all the way from the kitchen haranguing these poor people with questions even before they sat down. What's happened to good manners? Please, get us some tea.'

'Sorry, Daddy. Sorry for the sheer impudence of it. The Lord and his angels above know I didn't mean to be so inconsiderate. It's just that curiosity got the better of me. After all we have never before been honoured by a visit from the Dubes. We indeed have to make them feel at home, feel welcome,' the priest's wife said,

'I'll go and make tea for the visitors.'

'Count me in,' the priest said.

'Oh,' said Mrs Dube getting up from her chair, 'let me give you a hand, may I?'

'For sure.' The women disappeared behind the curtain, to the kitchen.

'I greet you, makhelwane,' the reverend extended his hand and allowed Dube to shake it.

'I greet you, Reverend.'

'Women of today are all the same. It doesn't matter if the woman is a reverend's wife. They've lost touch with their proud African culture of humility and good manners. She's haranguing you with questions even before she allows you to take your seats. Where have you seen such behaviour before? That's not how we were brought up. That's not how we are supposed to behave. We are not white people who discuss important things while standing, without even showing each other the courtesy of a cup of tea.'

Dube mumbled conspiratorially. As if he was seeing him for the first time, the reverend turned to Sizwe. 'Young man, what's your name? Are these your lovely parents?'

'Morning, Mr Reverend, my name is Sizwe. These are my parents, yes.'

'Are you one of those lovely boys who enjoy the company of their parents? Ah, good boy. I wish my boy Thulani could be like you. You know, whenever I want to go with him to the shops he starts pulling faces, inflating his cheeks so the face looks like a dumpling with too much baking powder.'

'Ja,' Dube said, 'children of today. They are just like their mothers. Always selfish.'

'By the way, my dear neighbour, I've never seen you in church before, even though I've caught a glimpse of your wife along the pews now and then.'

Dube wanted to say, 'What are you doing, checking who's sitting on the pews instead of focusing your attention on the Holy Trinity?' but he said, 'Aw, I come to church every now and then.

But in truth, I am not of the Anglican faith. I am a Seventh Day Adventist man.'

'Oh, I see. I see,' the man of God said, nodding, 'but why aren't you at church seeing that it's Saturday today?'

'Aw, Mr Reverend, too much of a thing is no good. God will sooner or later turn a deaf ear to your prayers if you persistently pester him with requests for more money, promotion at work, a good solid marriage, when there are millions of people out there dying of starvation in Ethiopia and Yugoslavia. God is merciful and all that, but he also does get irritated. So, what you do is you give him some breathing space, you know what I mean. Stop irritating God.'

The reverend grinned. He wanted to say, 'I'll remember that line.' But then he recalled there was a small boy with them. It wouldn't be good for his image as a man of the cloth to be seen taking tips from the likes of beer-guzzling Dube.

The women came back from the kitchen with a tray flexing under the weight of tea things and some scones. The woman of the house put the tray on a coffee table in between the two men. She filled one cup and placed it in front of Dube, who groaned internally but pretended to be taking a sip from the sugarless tea.

Then the woman poured for her husband, and then for Mrs Dube. The four sat down, avoiding each other's eyes.

The two women started drinking their tea. The men left theirs untouched. It's always advisable to let your tea rest a bit, to gather strength, you see.

The reverend kept licking his lips and swallowing hungrily. Finally he decided he'd had enough of this shit, so he turned to his wife and said, 'My dear wife.' He cleared his throat dramatically. 'I think my wife misunderstood me. I didn't mean this tea. I meant my own kind of tea.'

The wife scowled at him, but rose obediently from her seat and disappeared into the kitchen. She came back with yet another tray. Unlike its predecessor, which had been elaborately decorated with doilies and sugar basins and other glittering things, this new tray had very simple offerings on it: two bottles of beer and two glasses.

'Oh, Daddy,' said the woman of the house, 'I forgot to bring an opener.'

'Save your energy, my dear,' Dube said, reaching for the bottle of beer and using his molars to open it.

Dube and his wife exchanged glances. The man of God was thinking: Yeah, I think I'm going to like this guy!

Sizwe coughed politely from his seat.

'Aw, poor boy,' said the woman of the house, 'we've completely forgotten about you. You must be bored out of your skull. I'll call my son to come and fetch you so you can play with him out back.' She raised her voice now: 'Thulani! Thulani! Where are you? Are you sitting on your ears? Come here.'

Thulani, the yellow boy, came in.

'Yes, Ma, what do you need?' he said petulantly. His eyes widened when he saw Sizwe, the boy he had attacked, with the two old people who were obviously his parents.

'Thulani,' the woman of the house said, 'take this boy out back, so you can play together. Grown-up people are still busy talking grown-up things.'

The two boys glared at each other as they'd done not so long ago in the street. Then they smiled sweetly at each other.

Dube and the reverend were into their fourth bottle of beer, when the woman of the house suddenly remembered that the Dubes had come here to discuss something about her son.

'Excuse me, Baba,' she said, addressing her husband, whom she called baba, father, as a term of endearment, 'but I think we better start talking business. The Dubes here wanted to say something about our son.'

'I think we must call the boys in,' said Mrs Dube.

'Why? This is a grown-up thing. This is something between us parents about our boy,' the reverend said. 'Mrs Dube the teacher will tell us what the boy has done and we will take necessary steps to correct the damage, assuming that something wrong has been done by him.'

'It's not as simple as that.' Dube decided to break the silence. He thought it would be better to get over and done with the children's nonsense, so he and the reverend could get on with their talk and the cold beverages. He had not thought so much pleasure could be derived from the company of a man who wore a dog collar. Briefly, without pausing, he told the reverend and his wife what had happened between the two boys.

'How long ago was this?' the reverend asked, aghast.

'Ag,' Dube said, 'about a month, two months ago.'

'Why did you wait so long? This is a shock to us!' the reverend's wife said. 'This is a sheer disgrace, Baba. To think that we are such a holy family and we have a budding criminal right under our noses!'

'Call the boys inside,' the reverend said.

The boys were ordered to sit down next to each other.

'What is this I hear, Thulani?' the reverend said sternly. 'You've become a criminal, robbing people of money. And, worst of all, attempting to kill another boy by burning. What is this that I hear? Answer me.'

The two boys exchanged brief glances.

'Thulani, answer me directly now,' he said again. 'Why did you attack this boy?'

'Because he was rude.'

'Who started it?'

'I did.'

'Why?'

'Because I was trying make friends, but he became rude to me.'

'When you realised he wasn't interested in your friendship, why didn't you walk away?'

'Because Daddy said one shouldn't walk away from a problem.'

'But what was the problem now? He wasn't interested in your friendship and had every reason to keep his own company.'

'But the second time we met, he had money. I wanted to take the money from him.'

'What? You wanted to rob him?'

'If Daddy wants to put it that way, yes. But I wanted to take the money from him. You remember our electricity had been cut off that week. Mama had sent me to the shops to buy paraffin. I thought I could take money from him, go to the shop and buy a token so our electricity would start working again. You see, he laughed at me because I was carrying a bottleful of paraffin. An electricity token worth ten rand can go a long way, as you know.'

For Sizwe, this was confirmation. Their fathers talked the same language to their sons.

***

While many priests played holier than thou, the Reverend Tembe was direct – down there in the streets with the unholy, the unwashed, speaking their language, drinking beer with them.

A few months later, the reverend was to visit the Dube house. He sat with the head of the house in the lounge, smoking cigarettes and drinking. Dube's wife was away, doing some shopping in town. It was a Saturday. The two men sat talking openly about this and that. They didn't realise that the boy was in the kitchen and could hear everything they were saying.

'You know, Dube my friend, there are times I wish I could change churches, go back to the Catholics where I started.'

'Why did you leave the Catholics in the first place?'

'Take a guess.'

After brief silence, the two men burst out laughing. Dube was the first to recover. 'Oh, I know, I know. You couldn't stand the solitude of a Catholic priest. The celibacy and all that.'

'Precisely. You see, I am an only son in my family. If I were to die without siring an heir, the Tembe name would begin to fade away. I wanted to have kids of my own.'

'But you could always have children even if you were a Catholic priest. They do it all the time. Popes have children all over.'

'I know, I know. But I wanted to do everything legitimately.

You've got to understand, my father was never married to my mother. Wherever he rested his side was his home, a rolling stone, as the song says. As a result, I grew up missing the touch and firm hand of a father. I guess I wanted to undo the hurt that had been inflicted by my father on my mother and the other women he'd had children with. I went to a Catholic seminary in Ixopo...'

'You went to Marianthal, then?'

'Yes. Are you originally from those parts?'

'Underberg.'

'Oh, I know Underberg very well. Emakhuzeni, Bergville, Pholela. We used to visit those places as theological students. Anyway, back to my narrative. Just a year before I was ordained as a priest, I pulled out. Everyone was shocked. The cardinal cursed and cursed, saying he could see through the likes of me. We come to the Catholics in search of education and comfort, only to dump them once we had sucked them dry. We never ploughed back to the Holy Church. He cursed and cursed. Anyway the nearest thing to the Catholic liturgy and doctrine was the Anglican Church. That's why I decided to join the Anglicans. Theologically speaking, I didn't have to unlearn a lot of the stuff I had imbibed from the Catholic seminary. The point is, Anglicans allow their priests to marry. Anglican priests can smoke, and drink – just like the Catholic priests. So I joined the Anglicans. I don't regret it.'

'But you've just indicated to me that you are feeling unhappy now. That you want to quit the Church. What's the problem now?'

'True, true. It's not the Church that I am not happy with. It's the whole notion of staying married. Look, I love my kids. I think I have a great family. But I don't think I was born to confine myself to one relationship.'

'You want to roll on like your father.'

'Not really. I want... solitude. I think the Catholic Church will offer me the solitude I need. I enjoy being wrapped in my aloneness, doing things my own way, at my own pace, in my own time, without having to explain my actions to a wife, to a partner.'

'But, no, that's not right. What happens to the children? What happens to the wife, the family, when you go back to the Catholics?'

'I will continue to provide for them. I just need to be alone, to revel in solitude.'

'But that's unfair.'

'I don't know what's fair and what's not. I just have to be frank and honest with myself. I can't afford to live a lie because in the long run I might hurt the very family that you say I must love and protect. I need to go away, to be alone. Maybe that's my destiny.'

***

This conversation took place somewhere in the past, and Sizwe had only heard it second-hand. But he knew it could be true. People are like onions, his mother used to say, they come in layers. 'When I was young, if I made soup and I was chopping onions' – that's what she would be thinking. Layers, everyone has layers. You have to see them in yourself and in others.

Sizwe allowed his mind to go back to that other conversation, when he was at Thulani's place the day Sizwe and his parents visited the Tembe house for the first time.

'You robbed this boy because you wanted to pay for electricity for my house?' The reverend was shouting angrily now. He needed clarity from his son. 'You took money from this boy so you could reconnect our electricity.'

'Yes.'

There were tears in the eyes of the reverend's wife. She blinked repeatedly to stop them from flowing. The past months had been tough for the family, financially speaking. The priest's stipend was not going far enough to cover their expenses. The Church headquarters was under a new administration. Accountants had been called in to look at the books. This caused a lot of administrative headaches, which led to many priests getting their monies late. Congregations had shrunk as a result of the political situation in the country.

Political organisations were at each other's throats, their members killing each other. People who had worshipped under the same roof now held divergent political allegiances. Instead of bumping into each other on Church premises where they were likely to kill each other, they decided to stay away from the churches. Their absence from the churches meant that there was no one to pay for the sustenance of the priests and their families. The collection plates did not clink merrily as they had done all these years.

Dube, touched by Tembe's suffering, said, 'Mr Reverend, I suggest let's make bygones be bygones. Kids will always be kids.'

'You are right there. But my brat needs to apologise to all of us, but most importantly to your own son.'

'True, true.'

'Thulani, I want you to shake hands with your friend Sizwe now. I want you to vow before us, before God, that you will never never ever do it again.'

Thulani stood up and extended his hand to be shaken by Sizwe. The boys' eyes were full of glee. But the grown-ups didn't notice it. Thulani vowed to God and all gathered in the house that he would henceforth be a good boy.

'Good,' said the reverend.

'Good,' the other grown-ups chorused.

Now the reverend said to Dube: 'I'm so upset that the Chiefs–Pirates game will only be televised tomorrow, when I am in church.'

'You must convert to the Seventh Day Adventists so you can watch the Sunday matches on TV.'

The women looked at each other, and then at their husbands, with open disgust.

The two men cracked another bottle of beer. Dube said, 'Are you a Chiefs man, then?'

'Yuch! Don't talk to me about those moffies, man.'

Dube laughed, his tummy wriggling this way and that. 'I was only joking. Men of substance go with the Buccaneers. I am a Pirates man myself.'

'But, Dad,' Sizwe blurted out, 'you've always been a Swallows man. You made me a Swallows man!'

'Shut up, boy,' Dube growled, 'you haven't been spoken to.'

'Boys,' the reverend shouted, 'what are you doing in the presence of grown-ups?'

'But we haven't been told to go out.'

'Out!'

Five

Settling the Score

Outside, the two boys were killing themselves with laughter, mimicking their parents. Unbeknown to the grown-ups, the two boys had settled their score a long time ago.

This is how it had happened. Just days after Sizwe had been discharged from the clinic, he told his friends and schoolmates what had taken place between him and Thulani.

'The rascal must be taught a lesson,' the boys agreed. Sizwe was popular with many boys because he helped a lot of them with their homework. Besides, he was a good fighter. It was therefore always good to be friends with him. When all else failed, Sizwe could be trusted to use his Zulu fighting sticks.

Thulani, on the other hand, was considered a loudmouth and a snob. Because his father was a reverend, he had travelled with him to many parts of the country. Inevitably, Thulani bragged to the other boys about these travels and adventures.

Now, boys' rule number one is: Don't ever brag. If you have to do it, be very diplomatic. If, for example, your father has just bought you a nice pair of shoes which you want to show to your friends, always carry a piece of cloth in your pocket. Every now and then, fish out the cloth and quietly wipe away the invisible specks of dust from your new shoes. If no one notices, curse almost to yourself, but loud enough for those next to you to hear: 'Damn, these effing shoes are so tight. I think I better take them off.'

Now they will notice. They will gather around you and start pestering you with questions: 'What brand name are they?'

'Ag, I was in such a hurry when I put them on this morning, I didn't even bother to check the name.'

So you take one of the shoes off, and exclaim in mock surprise, 'Aw, they are Crockett & Jones! I wonder where my father got so much money to buy me Crocketts.'

That's the way to do it. But Thulani was not like that. Thulani used to say some politically incorrect things to his friends, things like, 'Have you guys spoken English to a real Englishman? I am not talking about these poor whites from South Africa who despise us. I am talking about real Englishmen from Britain. Anyway, my daddy and I went visiting over the weekend. A fellow Anglican, who's originally from England, invited us to his house for dinner. We went to the house in Durban North, sat at the same table as the white family. We laughed and cracked jokes. My father and the Englishman drank beer from the same beer mug. Us kids ate snacks from the same plate. When I went to the toilet, I discovered that the Englishman's daughter hadn't flushed the toilet properly. Her shit was still floating in the water. You know what colour it is? It's yellow. Not brown like a black man's shit. And it looks soft, almost soluble in water, unlike the brown bricks you guys expel from your bodies every time. Blame it on the damn pap and sheep's head that you so much admire. English people eat soft food that doesn't put demands on your digestive system. Their shit is therefore refined, just like their manners. The next time my father and I visit that Englishman I will invite one of you baboons so you can see what I am talking about.'

That was Thulani for you: honest to a fault. Or, maybe, brash and boastful. For that attitude, he was a sitting duck for punches and kicks on the school playground. So, when Sizwe told the boys about his need to avenge himself on Thulani, he had countless accomplices.

They caught him as he was in the middle of one of those long, enjoyable moments of pissing, his head thrown back, eyes closed as he revelled in the sheer bliss of the moment.

'Mama! Mama!' he suddenly cried out. Somebody had grabbed the base of his penis and was squeezing hard, harder. Somebody clamped a hand over his mouth to muffle his cries.

Then Sizwe showed his face to his erstwhile adversary. He started punching him. Then they forced Thulani's head into a toilet bowl. He was soaking wet, struggling for breath, when the bell sounded, marking the end of their lunch break. They warned him not to tell. Realising that the state of his attire – the blood-spattered shirt, soaking wet and torn – would raise questions from teachers, they quickly sneaked him out of the school premises.

On his way home, he had to think of a lie to tell his parents; Luckily, when he got home there was no one. He cleaned himself up, buried the torn shirt in the back garden. He got dressed in his casual after-school clothes and went out to the edge of the township where boys who didn't go to school hung around. He didn't want to be surprised at home by his parents. The questions would be too many. He wasn't in a frame of mind to answer, convincingly, questions such as: Why are you here at this time while other children are still in class?

He hung around with the school dropouts until the schools had let out.

He was making himself tea when he heard a knock on the front door. Opening the door, he saw Sizwe's face. He rushed to shut the door, but Sizwe was too fast for him. He said, 'I didn't come here to fight. The fighting is over. Here is your schoolbag.'

Sizwe turned to go.

Thulani called after him. 'I'm still not afraid of you, monkey face!'

'Who's afraid of yellow-as-shit face?'

They started laughing at the same time.

Six

The Abyss

Sizwe had been walking aimlessly for more than an hour now as his past continued to unfold in his mind's eye. He had been negotiating the streets of Hillbrow as if they were some kind of maze. It was way after eleven a.m. when he finally found himself crossing the threshold into Rich Man Poor Man's Pub in Hillbrow. He was hungry and thirsty. He decided he would have a liquid breakfast.

He sidled up the bar and caught the barman's attention. They exchanged greetings. He ordered a quart of Amstel and a chicken and mayonnaise sandwich.

Even at this early hour of the morning, men were huddled in groups, drinking, smoking and arguing. There was an old noisy fan hanging from the ceiling, recycling farts and burps that were being released with amazing generosity by the carefree drinkers.

Sizwe noticed that two men seated three barstools away from him were talking openly about him: 'Do you know who that is?'

'Some other bum. Why should I care?'

'Hey, that is Sizwe Dube, one of our greatest writers.'

The other man looked this way, sucked his teeth in disgust, and went back to his beer. 'If he's such a grand writer, why does he look like a hobo? What's he doing in this smelly place?'

Again, Sizwe found himself thinking about his friend Thulani as he faced the firing squad. But he decided to skip the details, and focused instead on what he'd done after leaving the Parade Grounds, where his friend had been murdered in front of ululating crowds.

He'd parked his car outside his hotel in Harare. He'd handed the keys to the parking attendant. He'd found himself thinking about his friend. Poor Thulani, he thought, why did he do whatever had caused him to be killed by a foreign government? Didn't he know that words kill? Words kill. Sword kills. It takes skill to kill with words. A sword kills without a skill. Sword. Words. Skill. Kills.

When Job used wrong words to God, the Lord answered Job out of the whirlwind and said, 'Who is this that darkeneth counsel by words without knowledge?' Didn't Thulani know this simple reality, that even God resents words used wrongly? Shut your mouth if you don't know what you want to say, or bear the consequences.

He was into his second beer when he saw a man entering the bar, getting himself seated on the other side of the men who had been talking about him. The man was Thulani Tembe!

'You are dead, Thulani! They killed you! What are you still doing here?' Sizwe shouted at him, and fled into the street, still shouting, 'Don't blame it on me, man,' running and running, continuing all the time under his breath, 'I told you to stay away from words and ideas. They can kill your mind. They can make them kill you. I told you,' running on and off the pavement, weaving through the crowd, talking louder now, 'Now you're blaming me. You want me to be you so I can die like you, with you. But I am not you, don't want to be you. Can't be you. I realised a long time ago I couldn't be you. I know you wanted me to be you. Tried to force me to be like you.'

He was breathing hard, yelling: 'You and your words and your ideas. Words. Sword. Ideas. Aside. Skill. Kills. I don't want. To be you. Or you to be me. Never wanted to. Don't infect me with your words. Your words are yours. They are you. Leave me alone, keep your words to yourself.'

Five blocks away from the pub, he slowed down. Sweat had broken out on his face. He looked this way and that again. He ignored the stares of people. He walked hastily and purposefully towards Braamfontein. Outside the Parktonian Hotel he bumped into an immaculately dressed white man, a typical Englishman in a blue shirt, maroon bow tie and matching braces. For a moment he paused, considering the man.

'Are you Thulani's Englishman?'

'What?'

'The Englishman that drinks beer with Thulani's dad. The black reverend drinking from the same beer mug as the Englishman who goes to the same church as the black reverend. Can I drink beer with you, from the same mug as well? Then we can talk. We exhale words. Sword. We explore ideas. Aside. Can we, Mr Englishman? for I am thirsty for knowledge. I know I am over the ledge. Hanging in there. Over the ledge. Know. Ledge. Looking down into emptiness. It's scary. Hanging over the precipice. It's dark down there. I am afraid. The abyss. It's black. Black mouth. Open wide. The abyss. It's solid, the abyss. I need to cut it this abyss open so it can swallow me. I will cut it with my words. My sword.'

The white man started running.

* * *

Sizwe's mind was clear again. The vision of Thulani sitting next to him in the bar, so real he even seemed reflected in the mirror behind the counter, had evaporated.

He was remembering how he and Thulani became good friends in the days that followed the interaction between their parents. They visited each other, exchanged comics and other adventure books. Sizwe was the fighter who protected his friend, Thulani was the flamboyant ideas man. He knew all the games in the world. He could make games out of almost anything. Both of them had slingshots which they used to chase birds around. There wasn't a variety of birds in the township, suburb, whatever. Only sparrows and mynahs. You can kill just so many sparrows and mynahs and no more. These birds were boring.

'Mynahs are the worst,' Thulani would say, 'they are as dirty as any animal you can think of.'

'But their colour is lovely, it's elegant,' Sizwe responded.

'You haven't been paying attention, I can see that.' This was true. After killing a bird, Sizwe had no heart even to pick it up and skin it like other boys. It was the hunt that satisfied him, the kill was an anticlimax.

The boys used to wonder aloud why other types of birds, more elegant refined kinds – parrots, loeries, cranes, kingfishers, robins – restricted their movements to the white suburbs. Had they also been fed the poisonous pill of racism?

The next time they killed three mynahs, Thulani picked them up and showed them to his friend.

'See what I am talking about?' He pointed at tiny creatures crawling all over the carcass of a dead mynah. 'The bloody mynah has all manner of fleas and parasites living on it. Unlike other birds which feed on either grain or insects, the mynah eats everything, including human and dog shit.'

That was the last time they went shooting birds. They had to find another use for their catapults. So they turned to street lights, taking pot shots at these until whole streets were plunged in darkness.

When they reached high school, they were lucky enough to be put in the same class. Sizwe had always been fastidious about his appearance. His school uniform was always clean, his shoes polished to a shine. Thulani, on the other hand, was slovenly in appearance. In class he played games. He didn't do well in any subjects. He only got by.

Sizwe, though, was always top of the class. Not once was he lashed by the teacher for failing to answer a question. He knew all the answers. His mother was happy with his progress at school. But he never shared the details of his school life with his parents. He established a simple contract with himself: parents will see only what appears on the school report. At home, he hardly spoke about anything. He lived too much inside his head. When he was not reading his books, he was writing stories of fantasy. At first he shared these stories with Thulani. Thulani enjoyed the stories very much. Without being dismissive, he would make one or two suggestions to Sizwe: Tweak the story here. Keep the suspense. You are giving everything away so early. You must make the reader feel compelled to read on. What's the point of reading a story when you already know the punchline? Why does this character have to die? It's defeating the purpose of the story.

To his amazement, he realised that once he implemented his friend's suggestions, the stories always worked. He showed some of these finished stories to his mother, who was highly impressed and proud. For a while he was happy with this arrangement, this collaboration with his friend on tightening the stories. But it then dawned on him that these were no longer his stories. These were Thulani's. Thulani's words. Thulani's ideas. His own ideas had been moved aside. Ideas. Aside. 'When I was young, if I made soup and I was chopping onions...'

In the end he decided not to share stories with his friend, not with anyone, for that matter. Not even his own mother. It pained his heart, for what is a story if you can't share it with another person? A story that can't be told to another person, that can't be read by another person, remains just a jumble of words and thoughts.

Still, he stuck to his decision not to expose his blindspotted mind to Thulani. In the depths of his heart he knew Thulani didn't realise that by helping him he was hurting his feelings. Thulani meant well. Thulani was a carefree boy, a free spirit.

Even with all the hard work he put into his schoolbooks, he found himself always gravitating towards Thulani. Thulani almost always had the answers, even though he didn't read as studiously. Thulani read a lot of grown-up books from his father's collection. But when it came to schoolbooks, he relied mainly on common sense.

One day they were doing geography. The teacher pinned a map of the world on the board. He would then call out the name of a place, and, at random, choose a pupil to go to the board and show the class exactly where that place was.

'Thulani, show us Uzbekistan on the map.'

'Oh, dear me, I haven't looked at my map in a long time,' he replied, to uproarious laughter as he walked towards the board. He had charm. Even the teacher smiled.

'Uzbekistan, Afghanistan, Kharwastan, Kurdistan,' he recited the names loudly as he stood there. Without much hesitation, the stick he was using to point the place out hovered over a spot. 'Uzbekistan should be in this vicinity, Mistress Mthembu.'

'Why do you say that?'

'Because these places Uzbekistan, Afghanistan, and other stans are in Asia. There are cultural, linguistic links between these places, at least that's what I've noticed from my readings.'

The teacher nodded, but warned, 'Pay more attention to your books. Detail is important. Common sense is not enough.'

But Thulani was not caned for failing to point out the exact location of Uzbekistan. He had shown enough intelligence and ability to think on his own, something that was respected by some teachers – especially those considered by many to be fair and intelligent.

Sizwe was amazed at this. He had known the exact location of Uzbekistan, and would have pointed it out on the map without hesitation. He had memorised the map, but had not been open-minded about his reading. He was learning by rote.

Uzbekistan, Kazakhstan, Afghanistan. 'Hey, what about Bantustan?'

***

Sizwe found himself a resting place under one of the trees decorating the open space in front of the Johannesburg College of Education. He wiped the sweat from his face. He immediately found himself looking at another snapshot from his past: the day after Thulani had been killed by the firing squad. He had been watching a football match on TV until he fell asleep. By the time he woke up again, the match had long finished. Some current affairs programme was now playing. He switched the TV off, wiped his eyes and yawned. His throat was parched. A nightcap was in order. He left his room and headed for the bar downstairs.

'We are about to close, sir,' the barman said congenially, 'but I can still take your order. What would you like to have?'

'Double gin and tonic.' He was the only person in the bar. The TV was on. His order arrived.

'Charge this to my room, will you?'

'Room number, sir?'

He spelt it out to the barman. He was deep into his third drink when six men walked in. They were loud, clearly tipsy.

'Good evening, gentlemen,' the barman said in a tired voice. 'We are about to close, but I can still take your order. Just one round only.'

'Ah, that's what he said to me when I arrived here a century ago,' Sizwe told the new arrivals conspiratorially. 'Grass has grown under my feet, trees have sprouted around me, but he still hasn't chased me out.'

The men laughed heartily. They placed their orders and receded into the distance. They found themselves two big sofas on which they ensconced themselves, enjoying their drinks which had been placed on a big lounge table in front of them. They invited Sizwe to join them. He said, 'No, thank you for your kindness, but I'm expecting a friend.' They let him be, sitting by himself at the bar.

The barman gave him another drink. Sizwe grinned his thanks, glanced to his left, and there was Thulani!

'You see what you've got us into,' Sizwe whispered angrily at his friend, 'they've killed you, now you want me to resurrect you. I'm not God. I am not a dog. It's not yet the third day since you died, in any case. You see the fruits of stubbornness? Stubbornness can only lead to pain, to bloodshed, to the gnashing of teeth.'

'No, my friend, you have to be stubborn in your pursuit of truth if you want eternal happiness. You have to follow your heart.'

'Truth? What is truth? You've told the truth, you've stood for the truth, but look where it has landed you. You followed your heart and where has it landed you? Deep in the dwang, my brother, deep in the smelly dwang. You are dead. Now you come here bothering me. Who do you think I am? God? You think I can bring you from the dead?'

'No, it's you that are dead. You are dead before dying. You are a nobody because there is nothing that marks you out as you. You are always trying to be somebody. You are always living in the shadow of other people's words, ideas, beliefs. That's why you are here. It's not that you love me, that you wanted to empathise with me as they pumped bullets into me. You are here because without me you can't be you.'

'Fuck you, Thulani. What do you think you are? I am a fucking successful member of society, a successful fucking writer. Do you think I want to be you? Who are you? It's you that want to be me because I am still alive and you are dead. So you think by becoming me you will come alive again. You think by infecting me with your ideas you can enter the essence of me and become me. No, I am sorry but you can't be me. Neither do I want to be you.'

'Sir,' the barman said politely, then he raised his voice just a decibel or two, 'sir, you are disturbing other patrons. You are making a noise. If you have to think, don't do it so that other people can hear it.'

'No,' Sizwe growled, 'it's him who started it.' He pointed to his left.

'But, s-sir, you're talking to a mirror. There's no one there.'

'You must be blind! This is the guy who's been following me. This is the guy who was killed by the firing squad today. Now he wants to take sanctuary in my body. He wants to come back alive through me. He wants to infect me with his ideas. Ideas aside. Words are a sword. Cut the abyss open. So we can plunge together into the dark abyss. You. Me. Him. The oneness of two in three. One. Eon. What does it mean? Am I mean? The lion has a mane. It also has a name. What does it mean? Beside. Decide.'

Hotel security was called to restrain him and take him to his room because he was trying to punch the barman, foaming at the mouth and screaming at the top of his voice. But they had to treat him with kid gloves. He was a valued customer, a famous writer, a regular who tipped generously.

Before he fell asleep, his mind was assailed by a startling lucidity again. Then he remembered the first time Thulani took him to Paradise Road, the shebeen in the neighbourhood.

Seven

Sis Lovey

A sweltering Friday afternoon. Three thirty, or thereabouts. It's more than an hour since the schools let off. By four p.m. schoolchildren are relaxing under the shade of trees. Oppressively hot to be scampering about the streets, playing football and other games. Tired of his books, Sizwe walks to Thulani's house. The yellow-coloured boy is sitting in a tree's shade, idling, gazing into the distance, watching the shimmering haze above the surface of the road. Lazily swatting at the flies bothering his face.

He gets up to greet his friend. His face is fiery red from the exposure to the heat. Almost like a white person.

They sit for a while under the tree, not saying much. After all, they were in class together not so long ago, where they exhausted their topics for discussion. They are sitting in the shade, not saying much, when Sizwe stands up energetic and excited all of a sudden: 'Let's go and kick ball a bit. Some guys might be there already, waiting for some action.'

'In this heat! You must be crazy.'

'Yeah, right,' says a deflated Sizwe.

With the help of the reverend, the boys had not long ago launched their own football team composed of boys from the neighbourhood. Their local side was called Exclusive Lads. There had been a heated debate over the name.

'Exclusive Lads!' Thulani had laughed derisively. 'Who doesn't know we are from Exclusive Park?'

'It's not about where we are from, but who we are. We are exclusive, you know. As in Select, Elegant, Unique.'

'What's so unique about an amateur soccer side from a

pretentious little township that refuses to be called a township? A township that thinks it's up there in the clouds. Look around you, man. Wake up and smell the manure. This Exclusive Park has got nothing exclusive about it. Even the birds know that we are a township. You've never seen a loerie here. All we have to be content with is sparrows and mynahs. Have you ever seen a hornbill here? Answer me! We are a fucking pretentious township.'

And then, suddenly, kindness took over. Thulani's temper was gone. 'Awright, you win. Exclusive Lads it is.' He didn't want to hurt his friend. He was catching himself most of the time exposing his friend's lack of street savvy. He didn't revel in the other's suffering. So the soccer team was named Exclusive Lads. They were registered in the Third Division of the regional soccer association. They did relatively well. The team was managed jointly by the two of them and their fathers. It was the pride of Exclusive Park. In the townships proper, youngsters had stopped playing soccer, wriggling as they were in the clutches of political violence.

Noticing that their suburbs remained relatively unscathed by the political violence which had left a swathe of destruction in a larger part of the province, housewives from Exclusive were heard to observe sagely: 'It's because of their refusal to find gainful employment that these black vagabonds from the townships are deep in this political madness.'

'Our husbands are working hard to improve their lot, to show the white man that we can be trusted to run our own things, to have our own governments running some parts of our country, but these barbarians from the townships are spoiling the good work our husbands are doing. They are all over the streets shouting stupid slogans, fighting against each other.'

'I say all townships must be fenced in with tall barbed wire, and members of the army should patrol the streets there until sanity returns.'

'I have always said that the black man, especially the uneducated variety, can never, never survive without the white man looking after him. We are like children, we need to be looked after, makhelwane. Let them sing about freedom till kingdom come, but they know in their heart of hearts that the white man is their God. They will need him until they go to their graves, and the generations to follow will also need the white man, amen!'

'Eyi, makhelwane, tomorrow is still another day for more stories to be told. I must go inside the house and start cooking.'

'Do you still cook? My husband is in charge of these peace meetings, trying to get the fighting barbarians to talk reconciliation to each other. By the time he comes home he has no appetite for food. The gory stories of violence that he has to listen to are enough to rob one of an appetite for the rest of one's life.'

'Hmmm, that's a thought,' the other woman said, but what she wanted to say was: 'You fool, your man has found another woman who can cook better than you.'

Thulani now gets up from his chair in the shade of the tree and goes inside the house. A few minutes later, he's back with two glasses of cold Coke. They sit and drink quietly, gazing into the distance.

Soon they are roused from their reverie by the sweet sound of girl laughter. Three girls are sashaying down the street, cracking jokes and giggling.

'Let's join them,' Thulani says.

'Do you know them?'

'No. But we have to speak to them in order to know who they are.'

'Do you know how irritable girls can be towards strange boys who accost them in this kind of heat?'

Thulani knows that his friend is shy in the presence of girls. He doesn't want to pressure him. So they give up the notion.

'Let's go up to the shops and hang out there,' Sizwe says tentatively.

'Hang out there doing what?'

'Just hanging. Watching the babes.'

'But you've just told me girls are irritable when it's hot.'

'Yes. But we won't be talking to them. We will just stand there, watch them as they pass by. Admire them. Just hang, man.'

'And that's it?'

'Ja, that's the general idea.'

They realise that the 'general idea' is not enticing enough, so they let it float in the air until it has been smothered by the heat.

Thulani says finally, 'Let's go to Paradise Road, listen to some music there. Catch up with Kokoroshe, shoot some snooker. It's Friday. The parents won't be home until late. They have to do some shopping, visit the homes of some congregants before coming home.'

'But our parents are sure to find out we were seen at Paradise Road. And are bound to be mad at us.'

'For what? For visiting our schoolmate and soccer comrade, Kokoroshe?'

The Dubes and Tembes had become very close over the past few months. They visited each other often, the men sitting and enjoying beer, talking about soccer and politics, the women talking about their children's progress at school. They also discussed Church matters. The reverend's wife had encouraged her new friend to get more involved, visiting the sick, giving succour to women battered by their husbands.

But it didn't go unnoticed by the reverend's wife that her new friend had a sharp tongue – especially when talking to her husband. In fact, on more than one occasion her friend admitted to having punched her husband when they were having an argument.

The reverend's wife listened patiently like the old sage and leader of women that she was. But later she shared this information with her husband while they lay in bed one Sunday morning before they went to church: 'I don't mean to poke my nose into people's affairs, Baba, but this Mrs Dube friend of ours is no good. Oh, no, let me not be judgemental. I can't say categorically that she is not good. But she needs help. We need to pray for her.'

'Why is she not good?'

'I didn't say she was not good. I said I didn't want to be judgemental for who am I...'

'Why is she not good?'
'We hear she beats up her husband.'
'Who's we?'
'Well, people talk.'
'Well, keep them talking. It passes the time, and it's healthy.'
'But it's not healthy to see a friend's marriage disintegrating. We should offer help early enough, before it's too late. After all we are the leaders of the flock, aren't we?'
'Let's say it's true that she beats him up. What's wrong with that?'
'It's just not done.'
'Says who? Just because you aren't doing it doesn't mean you don't want to do it sometimes.'
'What is this now, father of my children? Why painful words on a holy Sunday? Why verbal brickbats on the Lord's day?'
'People who express their feelings openly are better than those who bottle them up, whispering their dark prayers to the devil while they go about the world wearing false smiles on their faces.'
'Oh, father of my children, I think I have to pray for you this very holy Sunday morning. The devil sure is finding his way into your kind heart,' she said, and started sobbing.

He wrapped a towel round his waist and padded to the lounge. He found a glass and poured himself a stiff of brandy. Neat. Ah, he smacked his lips. He was ready for yet another wrestling match with the devil.

After that tough exchange of words, it seemed that the reverend's wife was visiting Mrs Dube more often. Especially when the men were not around.

The boys noticed this and thought their mothers were planning a major conspiracy against them. They had to be extra careful about what they did in their moments of naughtiness.

'Going to Paradise Road won't create a single problem for us,' says Thulani now. 'The old ladies know we have a friend there.'

Sizwe searches his friend's face, and says, smiling, 'I know there's more to it than simply visiting Kokoroshe.'

'Yes, but the parents won't know that. If they hear that we were seen at Paradise Road and ask us about it, we can always innocently tell them we were visiting our friend Kokoroshe. After all, that's his home. A home which happens to be a place of happiness for our fathers.'

'And happiness it is they derive from there.'

'You know, I've never been inside that place. Whenever I have to fetch Kokoroshe, I wait at the gate and ask his sisters to call him for me. We are in high school now. It's time we began exploring these things. Adam only gained wisdom by opening his eyes to the beautiful things that God had been hiding from him.'

'But where did that land Adam?' Sizwe says, impressed with the manner in which he had thought so quickly about that rejoinder. 'Adam ended up in the dwang.'

'But the joy and pleasure of discovery was worth the pain and suffering, wasn't it?'

'Thank you, Mr Poet. Let's hit the road, Pete.'

Paradise Road was the most popular shebeen in all of Exclusive Park and beyond. Celebrities, gangsters, teachers, ordinary people flocked to this oasis of joy every weekend. The place was run by one Ms Lettie Motaung, originally from Lesotho. She had come to South Africa in the late 1960s in search of the proverbial pot of gold at the end of the rainbow. She had settled in a number of townships around Durban, starting with Clermont.

Upon her arrival, she had found a job at a textile factory in Pinetown. She worked there for a number of years. To supplement her earnings from this job, she opened a shebeen in her rooms. Thirsty workers from her neighbourhood came around for a drink at her house. Some of them tended to sleep over, and were made to feel at home; she did not have a husband or a permanent partner to worry about.

Over the years, then, she ended up having nine children, all from different fathers. But the children never starved. Her watering hole was popular. It brought so much money that she stopped working at the factory. She moved from Clermont to a new township called

KwaNdengezi. Her new house was big. As a result, she was able to make an even more decent, even more elegant and therefore popular shebeen. She prospered so much that when new upmarket places such as Exclusive Park sprouted around Durban she was ready to buy.

When she realised she was ready to move into Exclusive Park she did an unusual thing. She bought two five-roomed houses next to each other. She tore down the fence separating the two properties, so that she ended up with an unusually large yard. Next, she demolished the second house, converting it into two entertainment outlets with separate entrances, separate toilets.

Because she didn't want to forget where she came from, she reserved one of these drinking halls for those drinkers who preferred sorghum beer. This was the brew that had helped her lay herself a strong foundation in the competitive liquor business. She called this sorghum hall Teya-Teyaneng, after her village in her mother country of Lesotho. Teya-Teyaneng was patronised up to that day by Basotho men groaning under the heavy weight of blankets, which they draped over their shoulders in an intricate traditional Sotho way. They were a close-knit community who preferred to stick together, playing their own music, playing cards, throwing dice, telling jokes in their language, or dancing to the music that came from an organ that took pride of place in Teya-Teyaneng. Patrons here preferred to sit on wooden benches, empty beer crates and plastic chairs. That's how they liked it.

Next to Teya-Teyaneng was a highly modern entertainment hall called Razzmatazz. This was furnished with wrought iron chairs and tables with clean tablecloths and a generous supply of ashtrays. Occasionally, the establishment distributed free boxes of cigarettes to patrons. In one corner there were two pool tables. There was a huge bar displaying a variety of whiskies, brandies, liqueurs, and so on. Depending on the mood of the deejay, the music of choice here ranged from deep jazz, to pop, to rap. Patrons drank a variety of beers, anything from Amstel to Castle. There were wines too. A variety of snacks were also served.

The whole establishment was called Paradise Road. Long ago, when Lettie Motaung was still a small fry trading out of her rooms in Clermont, her place had been called Sis Lettie's. All self-respecting shebeens of the time were named after the matriarch of the house, whether the husband was there or not. Shebeens named after the man of the house such as Bra Dudley's, or Bra Syd's, or Bra Joe's did exist. But they never lasted. Patrons felt threatened by the man of the house. It was the testosterone thing. Once the man stepped out of his house – be it temporarily or permanently – he wanted to go into a place that exuded female allure, where he would be smothered with the tender loving care of the hostess, where he would be made to feel like a king. People didn't go shebeens only to guzzle gallons of beer. A visit to a shebeen was, in a sense, like a visit to a shrink. The man would listen carefully as Sis Jane, or Sis Olga, or whatever the hostess's name was, explained to him how to treat his wife. Why his wife was sulking. Why his wife was now reluctant to have sex with him. Why his wife's cooking had deteriorated over the years. Shebeen queens knew it all, and more.

Conversely, if the host was Bra Syd, he didn't give you comforting words about your crumbling marriage. He would be very blunt: 'Get the hell out of there before she kills you.' Or: 'Beat the shit out of her. They enjoy being beaten because they believe that's how we express our love.'

It was for this reason, among other things, that men preferred shebeens run by women. The flirtatious attitude of the hostess was always to be counted on. Lettie Motaung's place in Clermont, then, came to be known as Sis Lettie's. When she moved to a better township, a better establishment, she decided to call it Paradise Road. In fact she didn't name the place, her hosts did.

Around the time she opened her new place in KwaNdengezi township, an all-girl group called Joy had released a smash hit single called 'Paradise Road'. The song immediately became something of a national anthem. It alluded to the resolution of South Africa's political problems, with optimistic lines such as 'There are better days before us... you must believe, you must believe...'

The song struck a chord in the dark depths of Sis Lettie Motaung's heart. At that time her business was in the limbo between success and failure. Because she didn't have a trading licence, she was raided continuously by cops who took away her stocks, almost driving her out of business.

She persisted because she could see better days ahead, and she did believe, she did believe. As a result she played the 'Paradise Road' song almost every day to keep her mind focused on her dream, to draw inspiration from its well of optimism. Initially the patrons were irritated by this song; they told her they'd had enough of it, couldn't she play something else? She grinned in their faces but went right ahead playing the song until it became almost part of the sounds you expected to hear as soon as you walked into the comforting confines of Sis Lettie Motaung's establishment. The patrons decided to call the place Paradise Road. The name stuck. The place became famous far and near. Sis Lettie Motaung acquired a trading licence soon thereafter, and registered the business in the name of Paradise Road.

A few years before, she had run yet another drinking place in Clermont, called Bitches' Brew. It was a chapter of her life that she was not entirely proud of.

When she finally moved to Exclusive Park, she didn't shut down her old place in KwaNdengezi township. It continued trading, albeit under a different name. It served mainly as a wholesaler where smaller shebeens and bottle stores bought their stock. She established a complicated accounting system so that officially the place was not in her name but her cousin's. The wholesaling wing of the business was making more money than the network of smaller shebeens she had established, under different names, in various townships around Durban.

Everybody knew the shebeens were the offspring of Paradise Road, but no piece of paper existed that linked these smaller places to Sis Lettie Motaung. So, she had no problems from the taxman. Sis Lettie bought new cars – straight cash. Items of furniture were never bought on credit. Cash was king. Sis Lettie would have laughed at today's young businessmen who buy cars on credit, whose groceries are bought using plastic money, whose whole destiny seems to be controlled by the banks. She paid for everything in cash. Which is why she was robbed a number of times by township thugs who knew she kept a lot of cash in her house as she didn't want to attract the taxman's attention to her wealth. When she was tipsy, she used to enjoy talking about the bad old days and how she'd made good. This was township wisdom. You had to let your fellow darkies know how wealthy you were so they would respect you – especially if you were not educated. But to the authorities, you had to project a humble profile because you didn't want the taxman running after you. The greedy taxman. As far as the taxman was concerned, Sis Lettie Motaung owned Paradise Road Inc, which was an entertainment club trading from some premises in Exclusive Park. Paradise Road Inc was in the taxman's good books.

'Hello, schoolboys,' Lovey, one of the older of the Motaung girls, greets Thulani and Sizwe as they enter the yard. Lovey was a shapely young woman in her late twenties. She had a deep brown complexion and a smooth skin. There were lovely dimples in her cheeks when she smiled. Many a drinker had emptied his wallet – just in order to be able to marvel at those dimples. After all, Paradise Road was a place where you came for respite, to get relief from the problems of working life; and you could equally be relieved of your hard-earned money. You drowned your problems in the drink, only to see them bubbling to the surface.

It was said that Lovey was as generous – in spirit and otherwise – as her own mother. She never hid the fact that she could drain four men in one night and continue to dance her feet off. To her, life was to be enjoyed. The more challenging, the better. If you were a jealous, possessive man, Lovey was not for you. A story was told of one of her many Romeos who, upon finding her in a compromising situation with another bloke, went home and hanged himself. But the rope snapped and his brothers fell on him with sticks. He was bringing bad luck to their home.

Now, Lovey is smiling at Thulani and Sizwe, showing her legendary dimples.

'Go on!' she says. 'Why are you standing there gaping at me like that? Is that how you look at your mothers? Kokoroshe is inside the Razzmatazz bar, preparing for the early customers.'

'Did you see that?' Sizwe whispers through the corner of his mouth.

Thulani turns furtively to look at Lovey, who is sitting back on a chair against the window, smoking a cigarette. Her legs are spread wide apart, her short cream skirt exposing the fleshy insides of her thighs. Oh, if she could open just a bit, Thulani was praying.

'Go on, schoolboys,' she says, amused. 'What are you standing there for, you yellow boy?'

The boys move hurriedly into the empty bar, smiling at the sudden growths at the front of each other's trousers.

Eight

We Know What You Did Last Night

'You guys try this.' Kokoroshe was offering Thulani and Sizwe a half-full glass of beer.

They each took tentative sips, knitting their faces in grimaces. 'Bitter. Very bitter,' they said.

'Maybe you want it cold,' he suggested, reaching for a can of Castle in the fridge. He cracked it open, took a long thirsty gulp. He smacked his lips in satisfaction before passing the can to Sizwe.

'I can see Sizwe has a flexible palate which adjusts easily to unusual drinks.'

Sizwe took a long swallow. His grimace was not as severe as before. 'Still bitter, but better.' He took another swallow, 'Certainly a better bitterness.'

Thulani took a sip. He agreed a cold beer was bitter in a better way. So, as they helped Kokoroshe sweep the floors, empty ashtrays and wipe glasses, they kept measuring and assessing the different levels of bitterness in the various beverages in this bar.

Kokoroshe briefly went out and came back with a teenage girl in tow. He introduced her as Nolitha, one of the girls who helped around the bar.

'Hi, Nolitha,' Sizwe said. The bitter beverage had done away with the inhibitions which would have prevented him from even opening his mouth at the appearance of the girl.

'Hi, boys,' she said. She was a sprightly young lady with a complexion as light as that of Thulani's.

'Why don't you and I get married?' Thulani joked.

'So you can make white babies,' Sizwe teased.

They all laughed. Her eyes were full of humour. She kept stealing glances at the boys as she went about emptying ashtrays, cleaning up the place.

By the time the first customers started trickling in around four p.m., the boys were very deep into the bitter beverage.

One of the new arrivals said to Kokoroshe: 'Kokoroshe! Since when are you supposed to be serving in this bar? Who are these other little urchins dropping slings of snot into our drinks? Voetsek! Out of here. Go call Lovey to come serve us!'

Thulani wanted to tell the man that he'd better drink his bitter beverage and forget about who was serving him because tonight Sis Lovey was supposed to serve the bitter drinks to the three boys exclusively. But Sizwe dragged him away into the darkness outside. Kokoroshe bid them goodbye and went about running his usual Friday night errands. He thought his schoolmates had gone home, but they had merely disappeared behind the bar, where they sat next to each other on the ground and started snoring softly.

It was much later, and a cold breeze was whispering in their ears, when they woke up. They were trying to get up when they heard voices coming their way. They held each other's hands and froze in their positions. From their vantage point, they could see two figures moving towards a tree, deeper into the darkness.

'We have to be quick,' the female voice said. From where they were sitting, they couldn't see much but could hear groans and grunts.

A few minutes later, a lone figure came into their line of vision, whispering, 'Where are you guys? You better finish now. I'm tired of serving drinks. Clients are demanding to be served by Lovey.'

Thulani wanted to whisper something, but his friend beat him to it: 'That's my father's voice.'

'If that is so, then my father's the one there in the darkness with Sis Lovey.' They giggled softly.

The two figures moved away from the tree to join the third.

'It should be my turn now, Lovey!' the voice whispered bitterly.

'Later! Customers need to be attended to.'

Once the three grown-ups had gone back into the bar, the two boys moved out of the darkness and ran for the gate.

'It's quite late now,' Thulani said in a worried voice, which was uncharacteristic for one so carefree. 'What are we going to tell the parents?'

'We'll cross that bridge when we get to it,' said Sizwe.

They laughed as they hurried home.

'That Nolitha is quite a looker,' Sizwe said.

'Ja, I think we need to check her out. Who should approach her first?'

'She must decide who she wants.'

They walked on in silence.

'You know, we needn't worry about what our parents will say about us coming home so late,' Thulani rationalised. 'Half the parents aren't home. The strategy is this: when you get home and your mama wants to know where you've been, tell her you were at my place. I'll say the same if I'm asked the same question. If she becomes aggro, tell her we were both safe, as our daddies were within close proximity.'

'Within groaning and grunting distance, you mean?'

They went to Sizwe's place first. Thulani stood at the gate, and deliberately shouted loud enough for Mrs Dube to hear: 'See you tomorrow, Sizwe. I don't know what's holding these old men.'

'Ag, you know them. They have to grope in darkness in search of solutions to our soccer team's problems.'

Nine
Death of a Giant

In the sprawling informal settlement of Siyajabula, just twenty minutes north of the city of Durban by car, a great man lay dying. Mdubuleni Mvubu was a man of honour, respected by members of his community and the central government in Pretoria. All his life he had been loved for his respect of the poor man, for his great regard for the downtrodden masses, for his sense of justice, for his help to those who stayed loyal to him, and for his decisive action and implacable punishment of those who crossed his path.

Sitting around his deathbed were four of his former lieutenants, each of whom held senior positions in their communities. Cyprian Mokoena of Port Shepstone in the south coast, Flavius Mthembu from Richmond in the Natal Midlands, Phakamani Zikhali from the north coast, and Phuthuma Mbutho of Ekuphumuleni, an informal settlement just outside the famous township of Umlazi in the south.

Mdubuleni Mvubu was one of the great community leaders who, when people had been displaced as a result of the political violence, moved quickly to offer the homeless people shelter. Coming upon a group of people wandering around the periphery of the city of Durban, in search of shelter and refuge from their political enemies, Mvubu had led these destitute people to a piece of unoccupied land. He instructed them to put up tents and other makeshift shelters. Within days, he had established a viable settlement. He used his own vans – he was a trader of some consequence – to help the people transport their water supplies from the city to their new homes. Next, he helped them make a dirt road that linked their settlement to surrounding townships.

It was tough at the beginning, but the people were happy at finding respite in this new settlement untouched by political turbulence. The settlement came to be known as Siyajabula – we are happy.

Many of the new arrivals showed an entrepreneurial spirit right from the start. They opened small shops, bottle stores and other small enterprises worthy of a new community trying to rise from the ashes of a political inferno. Mvubu extracted tariffs on all the businesses. Soon he opened his own bottle stores, butcheries and dry cleaning enterprises. The settlement had grown so big that every one of the small businesses had enough clientele. There was no need for rancour among the competitors.

The new arrivals were told in no uncertain terms that they couldn't affiliate themselves with any of the existing political formations. What Mvubu did next marked him as a genius of a man. Systematically, he went to the leaders of the established political parties up in arms against each other. Should you need soldiers to defend your turf, do not hesitate to speak to Mvubu, he told the leaders of the warring factions.

Soon Siyajabula rose to prominence, was reported on in the newspapers as the politically neutral reservoir where fighters – people who killed not out of hate, but out of a need to feed their families – were groomed. In a word, Siyajabula became the training ground for the best mercenaries in the country, thanks to Mvubu.

This was the man who had a sense of justice, a man who couldn't tolerate men who cheated on their wives, or philandering youths who impregnated girls and tried to run for it. It was from this crucible that the four trusted lieutenants of Mvubu had emerged. They had been great fighters who, when the time came, were rewarded handsomely. Mvubu helped them to replicate the concept of Siyajabula in other parts of the province. Theirs were communities of fighters who spoke the language of money, not ideology.

It was said, and no one ever challenged this assertion, that

Mvubu had strong war medicine for his fighters. Before going to war, his men would each drink three mouthfuls of war medicine from a huge cauldron. It was said, and no one challenged this either, that at the bottom of the cauldron was a human skull. After all, the fighters had had their fill before going to fight. Mvubu himself would reach for the human skull at the bottom of the cauldron, and also drink his fill.

The final step in the preparation for war would see each warrior – gun or spear in hand – being made to jump over a huge fire, while at the same time stabbing the air with his weapon, and shouting: 'Ngadla! I have hit him!'

Another story is told of how a young man from Siyajabula suspected of selling information to one of the political parties was summoned to Mvubu's house. As it happened, Mvubu was sitting in his garden, eating lunch. Like many rich Durbanites he always had his meals outside in summer; indoors was too oppressively hot. As usual, there were bodyguards hovering around the yard when the men who had caught the suspected spy entered.

The young man was brought in front of Mvubu and immediately started pleading for his life. It was so hot, Mvubu had stripped down to his shorts, his big torso sweating steadily as he speared a piece of meat with his fork, sliced it with his knife and took a bite.

'I don't know anything about selling information to the enemy, Baba,' the young man was crying his lungs out, tears streaming down his face, 'I never can betray the community. It is all lies.'

'Can't you feel it's hot enough without you spreading your spittle into my food?' Mvubu said, rising from his chair and stabbing the young man repeatedly in his left eye with his dining knife.

The young man collapsed on the ground.

Mvubu went back to his steak, spearing it carefully with the fork, slicing it with the same knife, and pushing it into his mouth.

It was a story that was repeated in many shebeens over the years to follow.

But now Mvubu was dying. He had summoned his men to his

home. He had also summoned the Reverend Tembe, his churchman of choice.

'I will die in peace, and with a clear conscience,' he told the men gathered around his bed, though these men knew he had been responsible for the deaths of thousands of people in the past few years, 'if my good friend the Reverend Tembe could be at my bedside to give me his blessings, to open the golden gates for me, for it is clear that I must go now. It would be an insult and a sign of ungratefulness to the Lord above if I tried stubbornly to cling onto life. I must go. It is only proper that I must open space for more leaders, for young blood to take over from where I left.'

The Reverend Tembe had honoured the great man's appeal. After all, Mvubu had been a loyal member of the Anglican Church. Although he lived in this great settlement of his, he had been a regular at the Reverend Tembe's parish. He donated generously. He was a trustee of the church choir, sponsoring all their out-of-town excursions. He was the one who had paid for the church organ. He had also paid for the uniform of the church choristers.

He had had a number of disagreements with the reverend over his methods of training people in his settlement to become hired guns, mercenaries.

'All we are trying to do, my dear Reverend,' he had once said, 'is to manage this political madness.'

'But by backing both sides you are only perpetuating the fighting.'

'I'd rather have my men involved in a real war, earning a living from that war, instead of turning to crime and other nefarious means of making a living. The kind of war we are involved in is just. When we attack, we aim for the leaders, not innocent and poor citizens. We aim for the political zealots. They must be made to pay for spreading the war psychosis. They must taste the poison that they are spreading around.'

There seemed to be some method in this madness. As soon as the Siyajabula mercenaries got involved, political zealotry seemed to die down. Leaders from both sides of the political divide – those who had survived the pogroms anyway – readily extended the hands of friendship towards each other. It was rumoured that the government had sent messages of congratulation to Mdubuleni Mvubu for covertly bringing an end to the fighting.

The province was at its most peaceful. But now that the man who had brought the peace was dying, people were genuinely worried.

If the many lawsuits brought against him were anything to go by, then Mdubuleni Mvubu fitted the dictionary definition of the term 'warlord': 'a military commander exercising civil power seized or maintained by force usually purely from self-interest and usually over a limited region with or without recognition of a central government,' as *Webster's Dictionary* put it.

But Mvubu was dying now, and people remembered how he had begun. A former taxi owner, he was on his way into the history books when he'd hit on the idea of Siyajabula. Overnight, he became a feudal lord.

When Siyajabula started, with no water and no electricity, it was the kind of place where mafia-type leaders thrived on the people's suffering: they offered shelter and protection in return for loyalty.

By 1986 population estimates stood at 120 000. In 1989, people from Siyajabula launched several attacks on the neighbouring formal township of Ntuzuma, driving people from their homes, some of which they took over for good. Others were burnt down. More space was needed for Siyajabula to expand. By 1990, population estimates stood at 350 000.

While at the beginning Mvubu had been a benevolent leader, later he demanded protection fees from people in his area. With nowhere to go, people co-operated. They were beholden to him. It was even said that when he wanted to open the first bottle store in the area, he went from door to door collecting funds for the launch of this enterprise.

Mvubu's methods were exposed when Sipho and Sara Mthembu, a couple in Siyajabula, brought to court an interdict application against the strong man in 1986. The Mthembus claimed that

Mvubu had threatened them with death and had banished them from the area for failing to surrender their son to be trained as a fighter.

When the Mthembus failed to pay the necessary funds in protection fees, they were summoned to the strongman's headquarters. The headquarters were like a military compound, swarming with armed men. The couple were verbally abused by Mvubu, who gave them an ultimatum: Pay up or move out.

On 26 May 1986, the couple were granted a court order restraining Mvubu from attacking or harassing them. Within hours of the granting of the order, a group of about a hundred people descended on the Mthembu property. Using axes and iron bars, they tore the house down.

The Mthembus disappeared. Just like that.

Even on his deathbed, his squinted eyes – hard, unsettling – gave you a hint of the coldness that resided somewhere in his heart.

His lieutenants watched in silent horror when gobs of thick blood started oozing from his nostrils and ears; when they tried to stop the flow, the man stayed them. As the gobs of blood hit the bed linen, they turned into huge spiders that crawled all over the room, then disappeared into thin air. Next, his eyes fell off, oozing with pus. One after the other, they landed with a plopping sound on the tea tray that rested on his abdomen – his back had been propped comfortably against the headboard of his bed. The eyes turned into two huge scorpions which wriggled around the tray, then disappeared into thin air. His skin turned scaly, a tongue hung out of his mouth, probing the air like that of a reptile.

The men took a vow of secrecy about what they'd seen. But they had forgotten the fact that in Africa even walls have eyes and ears.

Early on Friday morning, Mvubu died. As per the instructions he had given to his wife and his lieutenants, he was to be buried the following day. The Reverend Tembe was to lead the funeral.

So it was that on Saturday Mvubu had a funeral fit for a king. Political leaders from all major political formations were there with some of their followers. Religious leaders from across the country were also there to pay their last respects to this man who had given a lot of money to churches and charity organisations indiscriminately.

The Reverend Tembe's face appeared on the front pages of many newspapers in the days to follow.

Some young political activists and leaders were heard to whisper: 'This dog of a reverend must disappear. How can he sing eulogies to a warlord who threw our province into a bloodbath?'

Just days after the great man died, the story was being told in hushed tones at shebeens, at street corners, at taxi ranks: 'They say that the great man this that and this... but don't say you heard it from me.'

'Hhawu!'

'Excuse me for being forward, but is it true that the great man that this and that?'

'Hhayi bo! I hear that the reverend who was in charge of the funeral service has gone missing. Gone missing just like that. Poof!'

Ten

The Cockroach at Work

Kokoroshe was a chameleon of a boy. Not that he was slow like the four-legged creature. Instead, he had a sharp intellect and could easily change his character and disposition to suit his environment. During soccer practice, he was a tough-tackling, foul-mouthed, ready-to-fight, devil-may-care kind of a kid. After all, that was what was expected of you if you wanted to leave a lasting impression on your opponents. In class, he was a mild-mannered kid who submitted his homework in time, to the surprise of many teachers who knew that he came from a house that doubled as a shebeen, which translated into a dysfunctional family that couldn't be expected to encourage children to do their schoolwork.

In addition to being conscientious about his schoolwork, he always wore the right uniform from head to toe; naturally, his mother could afford to buy everything he needed from the proceeds of the roaring shebeen.

When sitting with his friends Thulani and Sizwe, he demonstrated a keen interest in and knowledge of the comics and books that they circulated among themselves. While those who might have known him at a distance thought of him as a spoilt snob who could afford to buy whatever he needed because of the money his mother made, at close quarters he was a humble, hard-working kid. He was energetic, with large round eyes that moved nervously like startled cockroaches – which is why his friends gave him the nickname Kokoroshe, Zulu for cockroach.

He was an avid reader, again an unexpected attribute for one who came from his turbulent world of cleaning a noisy bar filled with drunks, waiting at tables, washing beer glasses and running errands for his mother's business – all this at the tender age of thirteen.

His mother pushed him hard towards his books, rewarding him financially for achieving extremely good grades. As a result, he was easily the best-dressed boy around: Florscheim shoes, Dobbshire pants, Durburgh lumber jackets by the dozen, Jack Purcell tackies, you name it.

Although she'd not had the good fortune to go to school, she had long recognised the value of a good education; because she wanted her children to be better than her, she drove them hard towards those green pastures. Kokoroshe's elder siblings had all finished high school. The eldest two brothers had even gone to university. They had established themselves in the business world, deciding to start a law practice. Their mother had discouraged them from being involved in the liquor industry. They nevertheless dealt remotely in it in that they had, as soon as they started their law firm, taken over the books of the family business – on a retainer basis as their mother didn't want to give them a direct stake in the firm.

Kokoroshe, as a result, was doing well at school and enjoying it. He was a busy kid, his life revolving around school, soccer practice, his involvement in the running of the family business. Unlike many children in the neighbourhood, he never went to hang around the shops, making catcalls at girls passing by. He had a purpose in life.

But whenever he got time off from his chores and there was no pressure to deliver a school essay, he visited his friends Thulani and Sizwe, or they came to him. During this time they would talk about comics, soccer, girls.

One day – it was during the mid-year school holidays – he let his friends into the exciting world of making money.

'You know, you can make yourselves a lot of extra money in a very easy, painless way,' he said as they sat under a tree, enjoying a cold Coke.

'You must be careful of shebeen boys,' said Sizwe. 'They hang around with hard-drinking criminals whose heads are always full of ideas for scams.'

'No, it's quite simple, really. You go around the township collecting old beer bottles from the streets, from people's homes. We will pay you ten cents for each bottle delivered.'

'You think we can't see through this, huh? You have been assigned to do the job yourself, now you are passing the buck, huh?' said Thulani.

'In a way you're right. My mother asked me to devise a way to recoup all the bottles which the careless people of this neighbourhood have failed to return to us. We get penalised severely by the wholesalers for the missing bottles. But I thought that you, as friends, would be willing to help me – especially because there's money to be made.'

And so the three boys embarked on the great bottle-collecting campaign, wading through the sewers, going through the local rubbish dump, sometimes going from house to house asking for beer bottles. They had two wheelbarrows at their disposal for the job. To their chagrin, they discovered that many people were reluctant to part with their bottles because they realised that these were valuable, but still, they were too lazy to get off their bums and take the bottles themselves to a bottle store or to Paradise Road. Some of them were simply spiteful, as is typical of blacks who live in above-average neighbourhoods. You have to beg, cajole, go down on your knees for this type to co-operate with you.

In two days the boys had collected hundreds of bottles, and had been rewarded accordingly.

During their door-to-door campaign they had noted the households that had large collections of bottles in their back yards yet were not prepared to give these away.

The boys then started sneaking into these back yards after dark and raided the bottle collections. It wasn't long before the bottle owners realised that their stores were diminishing. Unlike ordinary township folks who would have confronted the parents of the boys, these upmarket darkies decided to do things the way white people would have done – they reported the matter to the councillor, with a threat to proceed to the police.

After a meeting with the councillor, Kokoroshe's mother gave her son a stern warning to stop stealing.

'Is blind, my broers, is blind,' Kokoroshe shared the sad news with his friends, 'the old lady said for us to stop or else. And you know what that means.'

The boys were deeply dejected because over the past few days they had developed an addiction to easy cash. They had shared with their parents the news of the profitable adventure of collecting beer bottles from the local dump and street corners – but they omitted to mention that greed had driven them to theft. Their parents had encouraged them when the boys told how they intended using the money to buy their own bicycles, like all the boys from well-to-do homes in the neighbourhood. The parents discussed the matter among themselves and agreed that this adventure was good in more ways than one: it kept the boys busy, but it also promised to ease the financial burden on the shoulders of the parents, who had for a long time now been pestered with requests for bicycles.

Today the boys sat there under the tree, each staring blankly into the distance, their minds working overtime. Their dreams of floating around the streets on their bicycles were within easy reach now, considering the money they had already saved from the beer bottle enterprise.

'I've got an idea,' Sizwe cried out, 'a brilliant idea, in fact. When last were you guys in Isipingo?'

'Ag, who goes to Isipingo? I don't know of anyone from around this neighbourhood who goes to Isipingo. Our parents work in Durban. They do their groceries there or in Pinetown. Isipingo is frequented by people from the poorer townships and the shanty towns.'

'You see, Isipingo is the logical place to go if we want to make money. No one knows us there.'

'If you are suggesting we go to Isipingo to collect bottles you must be out of your mind. How are we going to carry the bottles all the way from there? We would need a car. In any case, aren't we going to attract the attention of policemen who arrest vagrants and loiterers? Put on your thinking cap, young man,' Kokoroshe said decisively.

'Listen to this, broers,' Sizwe said patiently, 'the last time I checked, Isipingo was not a highly policed town. But it's busy. Almost every day you see floods of people moving about the streets. What I suggest is this: we get dressed in our most terrible clothes, mess up our faces a bit so we look like poor, hungry urchins, and stand at street corners, begging.'

'I think,' said Thulani, 'this is way out, man, way out. How about we go to the white suburbs, look for garden work there?'

'Have you ever lifted a spade in your life? Do you know how to use a lawn mower?' said Sizwe challengingly. 'I think my suggestion is strong and viable. No physical demand on us, no accountability to a boss. We are our own bosses, displaying our misery to passers-by, doing our damnedest to touch their hearts!'

'What! I won't do that! I am not a hungry urchin,' said Kokoroshe. 'If I have to beg for money to buy a bicycle I will beg from my own mama, not some poor strangers. I know my mama can buy me a bicycle tomorrow if she wanted to. It's just that I have not begged enough.'

'Don't think like the rich boy that you are, man!' Thulani said, warming to Sizwe's idea. 'This is not only about acquiring money for our bicycles, it's also a chance to live out their fantasies. How many times have we talked about acting out the things we read about in our comics? How many times have we talked about going around the streets, acting like private eyes, solving mysteries? Acting like beggars is an attractive adventure. It shows that we can use our heads, that we are creative geniuses.'

'The story about acting out our comic book stories was kids' stuff. We are now in high school, for crying out loud,' said Kokoroshe.

'That's precisely the point!' said Sizwe. 'We are now more intelligent than the kids we were. Let's see if we can be convincing enough in our interpretation of a comic idea.'

'Ag, I still don't buy it,' said Kokoroshe. 'This country is so full of beggars and other sorry cases that I don't think anyone will take pity on us. And what if someone who knows us recognises us?'

'Like I said, people in this neighbourhood are prissy big egos who won't be seen dead in Isipingo,' said Sizwe. 'Besides, we will have to do our best to disguise ourselves for this to work. In fact, what you've seen around town are adult beggars. A poor, hungry child standing at a street corner asking for money to buy a slice of bread will melt the heart of a poor sod who himself doesn't have much money to buy his own loaf of bread.

Thulani was getting more excited: 'In fact we can make our act more dramatic by contorting our limbs as if we're paraplegics!' He started walking, dragging his right leg behind him as if it were made of wood, his head tilted painfully to the left side.

'You yellow boy and your dramatics!' Kokoroshe couldn't help laughing now.

Over the next week, then, they practised their act thoroughly – contorting their limbs, learning to walk in a painful shuffle. When Sis Lovey wanted to know what they were doing, they said they were practising for a school play which would be staged as soon as schools opened.

When they were satisfied that they were ready, they dressed in their simple clothes one Friday morning, with each of them sneaking from their homes a plastic carrier stuffed with old, torn clothes. Then they went to the train station. Instead of going through the turnstiles where they would buy tickets and be allowed onto the platform, they found a hole in a fence along the railway track. Having crept through the hole, they would move along the track until they reached the platform where other people were waiting. They were not the only breakers of the law. Many adults who preferred spending their money on booze at shebeens were experts in this method of boarding the train without paying. It wasn't long before the train arrived. They got on board. Three stations later, they got off again, avoiding those turnstiles too.

Instead of going straight into town, they first went to the local dumping yard where they changed into their torn clothes. They rolled around in the garbage – laughing themselves out of their skulls – until they had acquired a malodorous air about them that would qualify them as beggars. Then they put on woollen hats which made them look old, haggard, completely unrecognisable. They walked briskly towards the town. Before they parted ways, they agreed to meet at the dump at four thirty that afternoon.

Always the most dramatic of them, Thulani started hobbling away, dragging his right foot as if it were paralysed, his head tilted painfully to his left, saliva dribbling out of his mouth. He carried a tin which he kept rattling, the coins inside making a noise which attracted the attention of passers-by.

He finally found himself a spot at a busy intersection. He sat there rattling his tin, saliva dribbling out of his sagging lips, his neck still contorted at an angle. Passers-by would pause, cluck their tongues in shame and hurl a few coins into his tin. Others, however, would curse: 'Damn freaks, why don't the police remove them from the streets?!'

Sizwe and Kokoroshe had hobbled in different directions. Sizwe found himself a place near the mouth of a subway which went under the railway track. Not only was he a good contortionist, he was also a good singer who touched the ears and hearts of passers-by with sad songs delivered in a tiny, sonorous contralto. 'Singabantwanyana abancanyana abahlala ethempelini. Usizi, usizi, usizi asinalo,' he sang. Then he would change to: 'Yes, Jesus loves me, yes, Jesus loves me; yes, Jesus loves me, the Bible tells us so.'

Later that afternoon, they met at the dump. It was deserted now, with all the fortune seekers who visited it every day having gone home. They sat and counted their takings, pausing to laugh and slap each other on the backs as they shared their experiences. They had each made a respectable amount of money. Their dreams of a bicycle were about to turn to reality. But Kokoroshe wasn't entirely happy. He recounted how, on more than two occasions, he fell asleep while standing against a traffic light. He almost fell to the ground, but luckily an old Indian man passing by had caught him just in time, assuming that it was because of his handicap that he couldn't stand.

They went home. The acting went on smoothly until, on the third day, Kokoroshe told his comrades he was pulling out. He just wasn't made to be an actor, he said apologetically. He kept forgetting how to contort his limbs properly and feared that watchful people might realise he was faking it, and could beat him up.

'I'm truly sorry to disappoint you,' he said at length, 'but I have another idea. I am good at picking people's pockets, a skill, as you can imagine, I picked up at home, in my mother's drinking place. I can show you how to do it.'

Thulani and Sizwe exchanged glances, smiled nervously, and said almost simultaneously, 'Sounds interesting – but scary.'

'There's nothing to be scared of. We are not turning criminal, we are merely acting. That's the name of the game: acting. We are acting like criminals, but we have no criminal intent or motivation. These past three days we've been *acting* like beggars, which didn't make us beggars in the true sense of the word.'

It wasn't difficult to win them over. They were obsessed with the whole idea of acting out their fantasies, after all.

Over the next two days, Kokoroshe drilled his friends in pickpocketing methods until he was satisfied that they were ready.

Then followed the next phase of the plan: they were to go to one of the busy shops in Isipingo and pick, at random, a person they wished to work on, a person who seemed to have money. They would follow the person at a distance and when they thought it was convenient – where there were enough escape routes – Sizwe, because he was small and agile, would rush forward and walk directly in front of the target. Without warning, he would bend as if to pick something up from the ground. The absent-minded target would bump into Sizwe's bottom, in the process losing her balance. While she was still distracted, Kokoroshe would come crashing into her from behind, as if by accident, in the process stealing her purse. It would take her a while to realise what had happened, by which time the boys would be gone. Or Sizwe would stay on, apologising profusely, while Kokoroshe got as far away as possible with the money.

The following day, a Friday, which happened to be payday for many factory workers, the boys did a roaring business. They didn't have to do any running as Kokoroshe managed to steal the money without being noticed. Because the streets were congested it was sometimes not even necessary to do their normal act; they just forced themselves into the throngs of people and kept their fingers busy.

Kokoroshe had warned them to lean more towards Indian women than the Africans. Indians, unlike African women, were bad screamers; if they caught you stealing from them, you could get away before their screams could be heard by those in the immediate vicinity.

'An African aunty's scream is so bad it can wake the dead from their graves, my boy,' Kokoroshe had said, repeating the words of his old brother-in-law who had trained him in the finer points of picking people's pockets. 'Stay away from the African aunties. Go for the Indians and the whites. But it's difficult to get close to the whiteys because they don't like crowded places. So, stay with the Indian aunties. Stay away from the coloured aunties. They are hypersensitive because they themselves are astute pickpockets.'

The following day, the boys were back in town. Seasoned pickpockets who knew the town like the back of their hands, who got busy mainly on Saturdays, soon realised that there were new operators on their turf.

Kokoroshe stood amid a thick crowd of people waiting patiently for a traffic light to change. Kokoroshe felt a hand grabbing him roughly by the collar. He looked up and saw the face of someone who looked like a tough guy, with a network of scars on his face.

The man dragged him away from the crowd, saying to him:

'I've been looking for you for a long time. Why did you run away from home, you little rascal? Your mother has spent sleepless nights because of you!'

Once they were alone, next to the public toilets, the man said, 'Give me the money you took from the Indian aunty in a red sari. And after that, I want you to get out of town. If I see you again, you're dead, bloody urchin stealing bread from my mouth! You and your two friends, I want you out of this town now!'

Kokoroshe, who had rubbed shoulders with criminals who visited his mother's drinking hole and had seen how ruthless they could be with each other, knew that the pickpocket meant what he said. He apologised to the criminal and asked for permission to go out and look for his friends so they could leave town together.

'Good boy,' said the criminal.

He had walked one block, hoping to bump into Sizwe and Thulani, when he saw an old beggar sitting at a street corner in a part of town frequented mostly by Indian shoppers. The old beggar sat on an upturned drum, holding a placard with the following words scrawled roughly: PLEEZ HELP HANGRY.

Kokoroshe suddenly had a brainwave. Smiling, he ducked into a general dealer's and bought a packet of crayons. He approached the beggar, tossed some coins into his tin, and offered to write a more legible, brighter and attractive message. The tired beggar shrugged, 'Ag, I can't even read the bloody thing.'

Just as well, thought Kokoroshe. He turned the billboard around and wrote on the other side in bold, black lettering:

NO JOB, NO BED
NO HOUSE, 20 CHILDREN
4 WIVES, STILL HORNY
JACUZZI BROKEN,
NEED SOME MONEY.

For the next few days the beggar was the talk of the town, with passers-by breaking into guffaws of laughter every time they approached him, rewarding him generously. Even the local rag used a picture of him on the front page.

The illiterate beggar wondered for a long time why his fortunes had suddenly turned.

'It's that boy with cockroach eyes,' the beggar muttered to himself, 'he surely was an angel from heaven.'

Eleven
The Argument

When the schools reopened the following term, everybody in the neighbourhood was envious of the three boys riding their red BMX bicycles. Thulani's parents were proud of his thoughtfulness. They realised that the long hours he put into the enterprise of collecting bottles meant working the whole day and coming home in the early evening tired and smelling like a dumping yard.

'It's a pity how our fellow South Africans go about littering the country, throwing beer bottles everywhere without even thinking twice about it,' his mother was saying as they stood by the sink peeling potatoes.

'Such a great pity, destroying the environment instead of disposing of their rubbish the right way,' he said absent-mindedly, laughing himself silly inside his heart of hearts as he remembered the Three Musketeers rolling gleefully in the dirt as they got ready to take to the streets with begging tins outstretched.

'You are in high school now,' she said. 'Have you decided what you want to study after high school, what you want to make of your life?'

'I want to be an actor,' he said, suddenly bursting out in laughter, 'I'm a very convincing actor. Hahaha!'

'Bah,' she said cheerfully, 'where have you acted?'

'Ask, tee-hehe-te-he, ask…!' he was laughing uncontrollably now, remembering his act on the street corners of Isipingo. 'Ask my schoolmates, ask my friends what they think of my acting abilities.'

'Stop this nonsense, now. I truly want to know what your thoughts are. We want you to choose a real career. Your father is not making money. He is even considering taking up a fulltime job as a teacher, because I'm not making enough at the furniture shop. We want to start making our plans based on your real ambitions. We don't want to do things at the last minute.'

'You know ma, I'll tell you the truth.' He turned to look at her earnestly. 'School sucks. I am ready to do what I want to do for the rest of my life. I don't need to go to school any more.'

'You can't say that. That's only the idealism of youth talking. You have to start thinking realistically.'

She knew that he enjoyed reading and writing. He spent hours holed up in his room doing so. But still, how could reading, writing and acting be one's lifetime vocation?

'But I am telling you the truth. I want to be an actor, I want to write, I want to think. I don't need to continue going to school to realise my dreams, Ma! I can write and think better than most of those stupid teachers at school!'

'Teachers can never be stupid. They are wise in the ways of the world. They have God on their side.'

'I suppose teachers are like wives in distress.'

'What?' she wheeled around, the saucer she had been carrying sliding from her grip and falling on the tiled floor.

'You don't suppose I am not watching what's happening between you and Daddy? He's hardly with you. And if he's with you, he's fighting with you. Look, I know he is under financial stress, but you are allowing him to use you as a doormat.'

'Stop it! You son of the devil! How can you say such things about your own father, about your own mother?'

'You forget what you taught me, Mother. You taught me to tell the truth all the time and shame the devil. Well, here it is, I am telling you the truth from my point of view. You, Mama, can't look out for yourself. You are allowing Daddy to use you. You are not your own person, you are always playing the obedient, God-fearing wife to fool your parishioners, but the truth is that you are suffering but are not willing to admit it. What would you do were Daddy to leave you? You have no education, and the money you're making at the furniture shop as a clerk is not enough to keep you going. But here you are pestering me about school. Look after your interests first, before you bother about me. T-Man has got his future all worked out for him, old lady!'

With these words he left the kitchen, bumping into his elder sister – the one who was in boarding school. She said: 'Why are you being rude to Mom, huh?'

'As for you, you better shut up because you don't have a clue of the life we've been living here for the past few months. Talk to your mom over there about her miserable husband, maybe she will understand you because you are a woman like her. But I am fed up, pissed off with people who behave like ostriches!'

He swiftly walked towards his bedroom, locked the door behind him and reached for his dog-eared copy of Mark Mathabane's autobiography *Kaffir Boy*. He had read the book many times, for inspiration not to lose hope that things would improve at home.

He picked a passage at random, and started reading:

> Despite being under considerable stress because of the bad blood between my father and me, I went ahead and sat for the Standard Six final exams. I had to do very well in these exams, for there was a possibility I could win a scholarship to help me on to secondary school. Under normal circumstances I would not have doubted my ability to do very well in an exam. In my eight years of school I had never been placed below the top one percent in any class. But the falling out with my father had left me demoralized and without confidence. I felt I would be lucky to pass. I conferred with my mother about my plight, and as always she had an encouraging word. She was the eternal optimist.

He paused and realised that what the book was saying was almost true of his current circumstances, except that his own household had almost broken down simply because his parents had no confidence in each other any more, but did not find it in their hearts to talk the matter through.

It was true that as a result of the waning support for the Church, his father's financial position was precarious. He blamed his mother for failing to serve as a crutch for the man under pressure. She had always been the one to be led by the hand, agreeing to whatever the man of the house suggested. He remembered that his father's parish while they were still based in Emthunzini, on the north coast, had been popular and well supported financially. They should have stayed there, as she had suggested when the man of the house asked for a transfer to Durban. She should have been firmer. Men like strong women, even he knew that, young and inexperienced as he was in the ways of the world. As it was, Emthunzini and many other rural areas had remained unscathed by the political violence which saw brother killing brother, congregations being torn asunder by deep-felt political allegiances. We should have stayed in Emthunzini, he kept saying to himself, but my mother was too weak to stand up to my father.

But he had to look critically at his father as well. Before they arrived in the city, his father used to drink, yes, but he did this moderately and discreetly. He drank in his own house, or at the houses of close friends, far from the prying eyes of ordinary people. Since they'd arrived in the city he had taken to the bottle in a big way. Not only that, he was now spending time at shebeens, mixing with all manner of characters – from shady car thieves to women with loose morals, as his mother would call them.

In the past, his father used to spend quality time with him, conducting mind-stimulating debates, sharing the wisdom he had picked up in his numerous books. He used to coach him in the politics of religion, why it was important to believe, but to do so critically – scrutinising the scriptures and relating them to current reality. He had enjoyed these interactions. But with his father gallivanting with the likes of Sis Lovey at the shebeen, he could only cry over that enchanted past.

Maybe I have betrayed my mother by failing to share with her what I know about Papa's other life? Maybe it's time Mummy knew what was happening between Papa and Sis Lovey? Perhaps that would light a fire under her apathetic backside, he thought.

Twelve

Dreams Wither Slowly

I've never seen my father so angry, Sizwe thought to himself, slowly pacing his tiny bedroom. For the past week our ducks have been developing sores around the eyes. Others are losing their feathers, and in a few days they collapse and die. Others develop swollen feet and can no longer walk about, quacking merrily, as they have done before. Then they stop laying eggs and we lose the steady income we've been making from the sale.

In the second week, Mandla, always the advocate for herbs, seemed to have remembered what he had learnt as a kid, way back in the rural areas. He prepared a concoction that was a mixture of the gooey juice from the aloe plant, manganese potassium, and warm water. Carefully, he forced the mixture down the throat of each duck.

Quite soon, the ducks, those that had not succumbed completely, began to show signs of recovery. They started eating their grain and laying eggs again. Customers began coming back in droves. The money situation improved at home. The tensions which had always been there between the parents, which had been exacerbated by the duck crisis, were under control again.

Until early this week, when the ducks started dying again. As Sizwe was pacing his bedroom, only three of the original batch of ducks were still alive in their enclosure. It being Friday, his father had gone to Paradise Road to cry his tears into a beer glass.

'Sizwe' – he was startled by his mother's voice – 'your food is getting cold.'

'Coming, Ma.'

'Come now, I can't bear to eat by myself, boykie.'

He shuffled towards the kitchen, where he collected his plate of food and joined his mother who was sitting watching TV while she ate.

A rerun of *Deliwe* was playing on TV. Because she had seen the series so many times before – had even seen the earlier big screen version of it – she decided to kill the sound and have a casual chat with her son. She'd come to realise that in the rage of his growing up, Sizwe who had been taciturn and a bad conversationalist, was becoming such a great wit. Why, at her own church, her friends couldn't get over the fact that she had a son who derived so much pleasure from helping the women who ran the Sunday school programme. Not only was he prepared to stand in for Sunday school teachers if they had other commitments on any given Sunday, Sizwe was also highly involved in writing some a cappella songs for the St. Peter's church choir. These songs were sung on special days such as the Easter weekend, the Christmas season, or during the choir's visits to other parishes as required by a national youth development programme designed by the church headquarters in an attempt to reach out to young people who were showing a growing reluctance to involve themselves in Church matters. Thulani and Sizwe were exemplary in their commitment to the Church. They worked together closely in recruiting young men their age to it. Their biggest catch thus far was Kokoroshe. This juvenile of unremitting delinquency had surprised his mother and siblings when he made it known that, whenever he wasn't busy working in the family business, he would go to church choir practice during the week, and church at the weekend. The three boys wrote plays which were performed both at church and at school. People had a grudging admiration for that naughty, arrogant son of the priest (these were the words of parishioners, some of whom maintained that the priest's son was proving to be like his own father – he was such a straight talker he could embarrass grown-ups who, in keeping with their Zulu upbringing, refused to call a spade a spade). He could write, sing, act – all of which took his popularity to new heights.

'I think that God works in mysterious ways is an understatement of the things He has done for mankind,' Sizwe's mother started, as she took a bite from her greasy drumstick. 'God is just too great for words, don't you think?'

Ummm, here we go again, Sizwe was groaning internally.

'I am talking to you, Sizwe. What do you think?'

'What? The dogs have upturned our rubbish bin, is that what you said?'

'Don't be rude with me! You can't mention the holy name God in the same breath as dog!'

'Ag, ma! You know me and words. I just like playing with words.'

'God is no playing matter, boy!'

'I'm sorry, Ma.'

There was a major shoot-out on the TV between the good guys and the bad guys. Both mother and son were momentarily distracted from the beginnings of their awkward conversation.

'As I was saying, despite all the hardship we've had to endure, God has been kind to us,' she said finally. 'Look at you, for example. You are doing so well at school that you've become the envy of our neighbours, who in the past used to say ugly things about you.'

'And you sometimes agreed with them when they said I was slow-minded.'

'I never said such a thing, my boy. Those words of yours are like a hot poker in my heart.'

'Ag, Ma, I thought by now you would understand my sense of humour. I'm just joking. I know the many fights that you've had with people who poked fun at my looks and slow way of doing things. The notes that I keep in my journal can attest to that.'

'Don't tell me you're going to write an ugly book about our family life,' she said, laughing.

'Keep on behaving properly, or I'll put you in my book.'

'Truly, son, I'm proud of you. So is your father.'

'But why do you keep having ugly fights with Daddy? You know, it's so embarrassing to hear stories about your parents fighting.'

'Sorry, boy. It's pressure. We are always under financial pressure that finds us fighting over the most stupid things. Your father is such a wonderful man, such a down-to-earth, humble, loving man. It's an interesting thing that his relationship with the Reverend Tembe has helped me get a new perspective on the man of cloth. I always thought he was a clean-living son of God, but now that I am seeing him at close quarters…'

'Mom, why are you telling me this?'

'Don't be upset, my boy, I'm only trying to share my concerns with you. I don't have anyone else to speak to about some of these things. I have to confide in my only child, who is himself fast growing into a man. My concerns about the reverend's lifestyle worry me a lot because they might have a direct bearing on my own husband, your father.'

That stopped him. His mind started working in overdrive as he wondered if his mother knew about the reverend's and his father's escapades in the clump of trees behind Paradise Road. Who would have told her? No, she couldn't possibly know, otherwise she would have long pounced – physically – on her husband and the woman concerned.

'People are talking. People are talking about the reverend's drinking, they are talking about his skirt-chasing…'

'Skirt-chasing? Why would he be chasing skirts? I'm sure Thulani's mother has enough skirts in her house. Why would her husband go about the streets chasing skirts? What's so special about skirts anyway?'

For a moment she was shocked. She thought her son was truly mentally disturbed, as people had been saying in the streets. But she saw that naughty glint in his eyes and realised he was playing games with her.

'Don't try to be clever with me, boy! You think I am a granny to make fun of? Oh, my son. They've already sowed the wrong seeds in your mind! You are now on their side, I can see!'

'Whose side, what side?'

'I suspect your father is getting up to some mischief with that reverend friend of his.'

'But how can they be naughty, whatever that means, when they are busy helping us run the soccer team, busy with Church work? They are always here when you need them.'

'Ag, I don't know my child. I am hearing stories. And these stories do not sit well in my heart. I don't believe what I am hearing but it bothers me a lot. I don't want to police your father, but where is he right now? What is he doing, wherever he is?'

'But, Ma, you are being unfair on yourself, you're being unfair on Dad. You know that on Friday he normally visits his friends. They sit, drink, laugh and enjoy themselves. He's been doing that for as long as I can remember, but you've never raised any objections.'

She looked at him, thinking how profound this son of hers was in the things he said. He was a keen observer, no doubt. If there indeed was something untoward that her husband was involved in, the boy would have caved in and told her. Maybe I should raid his journal and read it in his absence? – for that's where answers to my questions might lie. He is so religious about the things he records in his journal. But she decided against that ugly thought.

Meanwhile, Sizwe had receded into his shell of silence. He was wondering what would happen if he were to share with his mother what he knew of the secret lives of his father and his friend the reverend. He was into his mid-teens now, but didn't remember ever telling on anyone. Selling out on other people was frowned upon in the community. As a result, children grew up covering up for each other. 'When I was young, if I made soup and I was chopping...'

When the conversation with his mother was over, Sizwe said good night and retired to his bedroom. He reached out for his journal and made an entry: 'Life is getting complicated as I grow up. I've always been confident of my thoughts and convictions. But I am increasingly feeling intellectually inadequate. I can't make a decision before consulting Thulani. Indeed, I feel he is my intellectual superior. This is sad, shameful but I sometimes wish I were him. He's got an educated, sharp-talking dad. He can think on his feet, and can answer difficult questions at school and on the street without having to consult a book. I work hard at my books, I get the highest grades in class, but I still feel Thulani is far superior intellectually. And he gets the most welcoming looks from the girls. And everybody thinks he's the funniest guy around. I love him as a brother. But he worries me. Now his father is worrying my mother. I'll keep my eyes and mind wide open.'

Thirteen
Disappearing Acts

In the summer of 1989, Exclusive Park was rocked by a major development: the popular Reverend Tembe of the local Anglican Church disappeared. In those days disappearances inspired by political developments were quite common. The Reverend Tembe, in order to appease members of his congregation who came from different political persuasions, was decidedly neutral. He belonged to neither the United Democratic Front nor the Inkatha Freedom Party.

But politically neutral people were known to disappear. Some would be abducted by police under suspicion that they were activists of the UDF, which was considered a front for the African National Congress, which in turn was reviled as a communist, terrorist movement. Others fled into exile, where they joined the exiled liberation movements. Disappearances had become commonplace.

'But how can such a high-profile man just disappear?' Sizwe's mother was having tea with the reverend's wife. 'Someone must have seen him being abducted...'

'... or killed?'

'Don't think like that, Mama!'

'How do you expect me to react to this? We've been to clinics, hospitals, prisons. We couldn't find him or his body...'

'Which is why we shouldn't lose hope just yet. We haven't seen a corpse. Knowing the reverend's strong political convictions, he might have gone into exile.'

'He would have told me. He's always confided in me.'

'But they say men are extra-careful when it comes to political matters. They hardly confide in us women because they know we are weak, we cave in when we're interrogated by the police. So, in a way, by refusing to confide in us they are protecting us. It's safer to be ignorant sometimes.'

Over the next two days, the women went from clinic to mortuary, from one close family friend to the next police station. Still there were no signs of the reverend. Advertisements were placed in the local radio stations. A few crank calls were received, but there still were no signs of the missing reverend.

On Saturday the reverend's wife conferred with senior deacons about the following day's church service. A man was appointed who would lead the mass. Waves of excitement rippled through the congregation on Sunday, with worshippers giving the reverend's wife a deluge of messages of support.

The following week, she was summoned to Paradise Road. The owner of that den of iniquity wanted to talk to her about her missing husband. Having consulted her friend, Sizwe's mother, the reverend's wife said a few prayers summoning enough courage to face the owner of Paradise Road, the evil Lettie Motaung, who was known all over the province as a devourer of men, a breaker of marriages, a purveyor of alcohol and bad behaviour.

'It's your husband that I wish to talk to you about, as I told you on the phone,' Lettie Motaung said in a friendly voice. 'These men of ours!' She seemed to be at a loss for words. Unlike the foul-mouthed wisecrack that the reverend's wife had expected her to be, Lettie Motaung was courteous, even polite.

'Ahem,' she cleared her throat, 'I hope you're not going to take this out on me. I have been aware of where your husband is for some time now, but have been too embarrassed to approach you. However, I can't bear the thought of another woman spending sleepless nights over the whereabouts of her husband. I am a woman. I know the pain. I have been humiliated and abused so many times by men, the bastards.'

'Please, my dear lady, get to the point. Where is my husband? Is he still alive, safe? Please get to the point.'

'I will get to the point in a minute, but I want you to understand that I had no role in his disappearance.'

She started telling the story patiently, recounting how the reverend's disappearance had affected her own business.

Lettie Motaung was not the woman Mrs Tembe had imagined. For a start, she wasn't dressed in the sluttish outfits – miniskirts, high-heeled shoes, heavy make-up, blood-red lips, fluttering eyelashes – that Mrs Tembe had conjured up in her mind as she prepared herself for this trip. She wore a pair of fawn slacks that hugged her body without screaming at men to look at her. She had on a red silk blouse which exposed her unwrinkled neck. The only jewellery she had on was a bracelet on her left wrist and a huge diamond ring on her wedding finger. There was just a conservative smudge of make-up on her face, and she had on shoulder-length braids that were in fashion at the time.

Her eyes were those of a seasoned boozer who had had her fair share of encounters with the bottle but was now taking things easy. Her hands told stories about the rough life she had led in the past – first as a farm hand in her native Lesotho, and then as a factory machinist who handled coarse pieces of cloth day in day out, and much later still as a hard-living shebeen owner who used her hands to drive messages into the heads of stubborn patrons – both male and female. Stories had been told how she could challenge men to a fist fight – and win. She was equally competent with the knife.

As if she was reading the thoughts of the reverend's wife, Lettie Motaung said, 'One has to take some tough decisions sometimes. Which is why I am going to punish your husband once he comes back. He has caused a lot of damage to my business already.'

That startled the reverend's wife from her reverie: 'What? What has he done to you?'

On the day that the reverend disappeared, Lettie continued, she realised that her daughter Lovey had also gone missing. When she asked other members of the family, they confirmed her suspicions – that the two were having an affair. Now she got agitated, not getting to explain how the disappearance of the twosome had affected her business. When Lovey went, regular customers started complaining about the dropping of standards, the slow service. Lettie knew that it wasn't service that the customers were complaining about; it was Lovey's presence that they missed. Lovey was good at making customers feel good about themselves. She had mastered the art of flirting just as her mother had done those many years ago. Not only was she a good flirt, she also was good-looking. And generous too. When the mood took her, she would ply customers with free drinks now and then – not causing even a dent in the profits because the drinks were overpriced as it was. Besides, regular customers tipped lavishly.

Nolitha, the other girl who served drinks at the bar, was also good. But she was still too young and inexperienced, or simply not gifted enough to help men relieve themselves of their hard-earned cash. She always knew that her daughter, wherever she was, was safe. In this daughter of hers she saw a lot of herself. She remembered that, as a younger woman, she had enjoyed this game of disappearing – especially when she was briefly married to one of the top gangsters in town.

Anyway, three days after Lovey went missing, the story went on, Lettie had felt under such immense pressure that she decided to get out of hibernation, to go and play hostess herself now that her wayward daughter had disappeared. It was a Friday night when Lettie decided to make her first appearance in many years in her own club. Razzmatazz was beginning to fill up with the regular customers, who were feeding their hearts with the hope that their favourite hostess Lovey would make her appearance. They kept wondering aloud: 'Is Lovey in today? What the fuck happened to Lovey?'

* * *

Then an apparition, a thing from heaven, appeared at the entrance to the club. She was tall on her silver stiletto heels, sparkling in a red sleeveless evening dress. She had on gloves that reached to her elbows. Large earrings dangled from her lobes, their beauty enhanced by a dark Diana Ross wig she had on.

There were murmurs: 'Who's this?'

'Abigail Kubheka,' some knowledgeable Johns offered, mistaking her for the famous cabaret singer.

'Sheeeit! Is she going to sing then?'

'Dammit! This is Lovey!' one man said, getting up from his seat and coming this way. 'No sheeeit! It's the ol' lady herself, Sis Lettie.' The man got weak in his knees.

'Hello, boys, having a good time?' Lettie said in her cheerful voice.

'Sis Lettie! Sis Lettie!'

Younger men who had never laid eyes on her decided there and then that Lovey could stay away from here as long as she wanted; this thing of beauty, this apparition of perfection in front of them, was miles ahead of Lovey.

Older men, some of whom had sampled the pleasures of this lovely matron, felt pangs of hunger inside them. They groaned longingly as they recalled her warmth from days past. They wanted to be smothered in her charm. Lovey could stay away if she wanted to, they decided. Lettie had matured like good wine – to perfection. In fact she surpassed perfection. She was in the realm of goddesses. Women who were sitting with the men glared at the drooling fools, plying them with more drinks. Others walked angrily to the bathrooms, where they stood in front of the mirror and started freshening up their make-up and dabbing their lips with lip gloss.

'Who's this bitch who's just come in?'

'Oh, I hear she's some famous singing whore.'

'No, in fact she is the owner of the joint.'

'I always thought the owner was some old crone!'

'Obviously not. Better pull up your socks, doll!'

'Or she's going to pull your man by his dick.'

'Imagine going home by yourself!'

They giggled, and went back to the club, gladiators ready for the fight.

Back in the club, the deejay stopped playing Brenda Fassie and put on the queen's favourite, 'Paradise Road':

Come with me down Paradise Road
This way please, I'll carry your load
This you won't believe
Come with me to paradise skies
Look outside, and open your eyes
This you must believe
There are better days before us...'

Now the house was rocking, with men who had no women hugging themselves and staring dreamily into the glittering ceiling as they moved slowly to the music, recalling the warm embraces of women they hungered after, the women they wished to confide their undying love to but were afraid to do so.

After 'Paradise Road', the house succumbed to the sounds of Anita Baker's 'Body and Soul'.

Patrons were surprised when the waitresses invaded their tables, plying them with drinks.

'No, but I didn't order this!'

'It's on the house, honey!'

Not so much booze had been consumed in a long time in one night. People talked about it at the soccer stadium, in trains, in taxis. People started flocking back to Paradise Road to sample the delights of the hostess.

* * *

'You see, now,' Lettie continued to tell the story to the reverend's wife, 'this is the kind of life I used to enjoy as a younger woman. But your husband, who has decided to gallivant with my daughter, is forcing me to do time travel, to go to a past I thought I was done with, or my customers will run away and my business will go under. Now, woman to woman, I know you have nothing to do with your husband's behaviour. I know the two of them will be coming back sooner or later. But I want you to assure me: Once he is back, you'll make sure he doesn't come any closer to my daughter, or I will be tempted to confront him myself. And, let me assure you, you don't want that to happen.'

Fourteen
The Release

'The problem with people who don't read books carefully,' Sizwe was telling his friends Thulani and Kokoroshe, 'is that they fail to appreciate important milestones in our history.'

'What's historical about Nelson Mandela's release?' Thulani was uncharacteristically impatient, refusing to see the logic in the celebrations that were taking place all over the country as black South Africa celebrated the release of Mandela. 'Mandela did fuckall for you and me. In fact his release is the beginning of a long process of betrayal of our cause. He was released on their own terms, on the terms of the white world.'

'Of course no one is saying Mandela was the be-all and end-all of our struggle,' Kokoroshe ventured, 'but he is an important symbol of it. The struggle, which has brought the apartheid government to its knees, was given impetus by the Release Mandela Campaign. But of course no single individual holds the key to our liberation, not Mandela, not the name of Steve Biko, not Sisulu...'

'Those are wise words, my boy,' said a patron who had been listening to the boys who sat under the tree outside the Razzmatazz Club. 'I'm amazed that such small boys as you are having such an adult discussion. I take it you are schoolboys. What standards are you in now?'

'Standard Nine.'

'Wow! I am truly impressed. Not even university graduates can articulate the meaning of our struggle as well as you are doing. Anyway, as much as some of us are of the Black Consciousness tradition, we cannot underestimate the contributions which have been made by the Charterists, the Africanists, even Inkatha.'

The three young men looked at each other and wanted to burst out laughing. They thought better of it.

Just then, Nolitha walked out of the club carrying a bucket and a broom. Even in her work clothes she looked stunning, wearing jeans that were torn at strategic places, exposing patches of her light-complexioned thighs.

'Litha!' said Thulani, 'How are you, sweetie pie?'

'I am cool, honey bunch.'

The boys murmured admiration, attracting a disapproving glance from the man who was drinking his beer.

Throughout their stay at Kokoroshe's place, Sizwe couldn't help noticing that his friend Thulani was angry. Ever since the disappearance of his father and the rumours that followed, he had been like a wound spring. He initiated debates he couldn't win. He was moody. For the first time, Sizwe felt intellectually superior to his friend. This made him feel good and bad. Good because ever since they'd been kids he'd always played second fiddle to his friend, be it on the sporting field, on the debating floor, in the street, in their interactions with girls. But it made him feel bad because he had not realised, in so many words, that he had such an inferiority complex. He groaned in disgust at the unworthy thoughts he entertained against his friend.

It was late in the afternoon when Nolitha knocked off from her work. Thulani offered to walk her home. She agreed happily. Sizwe had been eager to go home so he could indulge himself in a new collection of comics his mom had brought back a few days ago. He also felt the urge to make a few entries in his journal. But when Thulani asked him if he wanted to come too, to accompany Nolitha, he agreed readily.

On the way towards Nolitha's home – she lived in one of the shacks on the edge of Exclusive Park – the three young people spoke about everything from the latest music to the fancy cars they kept coming across. It didn't go unnoticed to Sizwe that his two companions were now holding hands. Nolitha seemed to be enjoying this immensely. Now and then Thulani tickled her rib cage. Instead of fobbing him off, she giggled with unmasked joy. Demarcating Exclusive Park from the shackland where Nolitha lived was a stretch of no man's land. This was covered by tall grass and clumps of trees. The dirt road they were using cut a meandering swathe through this thick undergrowth.

'I think I must turn back home now,' said Sizwe, 'I'll see you guys tomorrow.'

'Come on, Sizwe,' Nolitha said, 'you can't leave us halfway.'

When they were in the middle of the dirt road, Thulani and Nolitha slackened their pace and started kissing. Sizwe got nervous. What if a grown-up appeared and saw what was happening?

Thulani and Nolitha seemed to be reading his mind because, still hand in hand, they waded through the tall grass, further into the undergrowth, until Sizwe couldn't see their heads. He stood in the middle of dirt road, looking this and that way, panicking.

It was getting dark when Thulani emerged from the undergrowth, a huge smile on his face: 'She's ready for you.'

Without hesitation, Sizwe joined Nolitha on a nest of leaves and grass.

After they'd dropped her safely at her parents' place, they walked home, an unmistakable spring in their step. When Sizwe got home, he went straight into his bedroom. When his mother offered him a plate of food, he rejected it.

In his journal, he wrote: 'I am tired of this. I feel dirty. This is disgusting. I feel inferior. I feel belittled. Why is it that I always come after Thulani? His father seems to be leading the way, while mine follows. Why is this so? Are we inferior to them? Is there something wrong in our intellectual make-up?' It was a question that would keep popping up in his mind in the years to follow.

As an afterthought, he made the following entry: 'I lost my virginity on the same day that Mandela was released from prison. Any significant meaning behind this?'

He laughed out loud until his mother poked her head into his bedroom: 'Are you all right?'

'Mandela's release has made me a mature, happy young man!'

Fifteen
Blood Brothers

'We've had a good time, babe,' Lovey was talking to the Reverend Tembe in their hide-out in one of the sumptuous lodges along the Wild Coast. 'But I think we have to go back home now. Enough is enough.'

'Can't we stay a bit longer? I just can't get enough of you. I think I was destined to be yours. You are my sustenance.'

'You have a family to go back to. My mother must be seething, she needs me home to come and take control of the business. My siblings are busy with their own shit, they don't have enough time to help Mama with Paradise Road. For her part, my mama is too tired for this kind of shit, bless her.'

Having just taken a shower, she was all naked but for a white G-string, and was walking about the spacious room gathering her things and carefully packing them into a suitcase. He was lying in bed, sipping champagne from a fluted glass. They had been spoiling themselves with cheese and champagne breakfasts since their arrival here.

'Sweetie, you can't drag me away from my wife and dump me here.'

'I am not dumping you here. I am telling you very simply: Let's go back home. To Paradise Road where the fun never sets.'

'This is no time for light-hearted banter. I finished with my wife, I've told you numerous times. My life is with you forever and ever, Amen.'

'Don't you give me that biblical shit now. I never gave you my hand in marriage, your wife did. You owe it to her, your family and your congregation to do the right thing. Go home. If you don't want to go, I'll leave you here, I promise you.'

'How can you do this to me?' Tears were running down his face now.

'What have I done? Stop behaving like a kid. Be a man with balls. Go home and face the music. Isn't that what you preach to members of your congregation, to be strong enough to make peace with their Gods, to love and treasure their families?'

'What does this all mean? Is this the end of us now? What has happened to the promises you made to me, to love and protect me, to pick me up every time I fall?'

She glared at him for a few moments, clambered into her jeans and clicked her tongue in disgust. 'Enough of your shit now. Get out of that bed and let's go.'

***

'Since when have you started visiting my house, you?' Thulani was glaring at Archdeacon Bhengu, who was standing at the door, ready to gain entry to the house. 'It's not even a month since my father turned his back on my mother, now you're all drooling after her.'

'Is this what the reverend taught you, my son?' the grey-haired deacon said in a hurt tone. 'Here I am, standing at the door of your parents, ready to offer succour to your poor mother, and all you're intent on doing is to heap insults upon me!'

'Your succour sucks!'

His mother appeared like a whirlwind, punching the boy out of the way. He crashed against the door jamb, fell to the ground.

'Come in, deacon, this son of the devil has been tempting my patience for a long time now,' she said.

The archdeacon stepped over the prone figure of the boy.

Thulani got up slowly and walked to the back of the house where he sat down on the lawn, grinding his jaws, his mind saddled with an ugly mess in his head. His was a pain both physical and emotional. He was missing his father, and felt even more saddened that the men from the Church were running after his mother like hungry hounds. But more pressing was the physical pain.

Two days after his sexual encounter with Nolitha, he had begun to have a searing sensation around his penis whenever he tried to take a leak. A day later, suppurating sores sprang up around his groin. One day, taking a leak, he was seen by some of his classmates gripping the top of the urinal, his head thrown back in sheer agony.

'Hey, somebody's got the drop,' the boys teased.

'Finally crossed the Rubicon, hey, boy.'

The boys crowded around him: 'Show us! Show us!'

They looked at his mutilated member and wrinkled their noses. One of the bigger boys was only interested in the size: 'Is that all you've got? You Zulu boys are miserable. Such a tiny thing. Watch this.' He showed them his own Bob Fella, as he preferred to call his thingie.

'But you Shangaans are miserable,' one of the boys cried out. 'Such a fully rounded manly dick, and it has never tasted a woman!'

They laughed.

Later, Thulani conferred with his friend Sizwe. Turned out the latter had been suffering in silence, ashamed to tell his friend that he had contracted venereal disease as well.

'But don't worry, my father will set us straight. He knows all the herbs to take care of minor inconveniences.'

'Have you told him yet?'

'Of course, I couldn't bear the pain any more. I just had to tell him.'

Thulani stood there in front of his friend, his heart aching. Where was his own father when he needed him most? Sizwe urged him to visit him at his place and explain his predicament to Mr Dube, who was familiar with all the herbs in the world.

When the two boys limped about, dangling their mutilated members between their legs, Sizwe realised that he was linked by fate to his friend Thulani, that the gods wanted them to be together in their happiness and suffering, that they were indeed blood brothers. Privately he felt superior to his friend because his own father knew herbs that would help both of them.

As Thulani sat there on the grass, deep in his own thoughts, he felt useless. As the eldest boy, he felt, he should be there comforting his mother. His outspoken father had on many occasions taught him to be strong, to be always there to offer a shoulder to cry on – to his mother, to his sisters. But where was his father now with all his noble words and thoughts? Was he not the one who had started all the problems, was he not the source of all his mother's suffering? Was he to be trusted again after this?

He wondered what he would do if his father appeared right now.

Sixteen
Make-Believe

Sizwe was deep into one of his make-believe stories he had started writing a few days previously. When he paused and sat back comfortably in his bed, he was shocked at the realisation. Although he had authored the story himself, its meaning came as a surprise to him as he started reading it.

The story was about two families who are friendly with each other, go to the same church, and live in the same neighbourhood. In the story one of the two heads of families is a successful lawyer and his wife a teacher. The father is a well-known womaniser who has on two occasions been struck off the roll of lawyers for his corrupt conduct, but on appeal he wins back his position on the roll. This father is rich but careless. In his drunken binges, he has crashed three cars in a space of two years. The lawyer and the teacher have a spoilt brat of a son who, although he is not doing well at school, is loved by neighbours, schoolmates, teachers, people at church. He is very dark in complexion, with flared nostrils, as ugly as if God made him when he was in a bad mood.

Meanwhile, the head of the other family is a hard-working bricklayer who has a foul-mouthed wife, another teacher. The man's major vice is that he spends all his wages on a lousy third-division soccer team. When his wife complains and threatens him with divorce, he says patiently, 'Kaizer Motaung and Jomo Sono are successful soccer barons today because they worked hard. They had to start somewhere before they climbed to where they are today. They spent a lot of their money right at the beginning, now they are reaping the benefits.'

The family lives frugally, yet can barely afford to send their son to one of the upper-class black high schools. The son is quietly intelligent but afraid of everything from girls to failing his tests. As a result, he is a studious little bore – or so other people think. Although he is good-looking, with a light skin and curly hair (thanks to his mother's coloured heritage), he is never successful with girls. Girls only get to speak to him at the say-so of his ugly, spoilt-brat friend.

At some stage the lawyer decides to invest some money in his bricklayer friend's soccer team. The team is suddenly successful, moving to the top of the third-division league. Then the following year it is promoted to the second division, and then the first. Sponsorships started flowing in. The two men are now relatively well off from the money generated by the soccer team. Because of his education, the lawyer assumes control of the club – even though he continues to share the spoils fairly with his bricklayer friend.

But the lawyer gradually sinks deeper into his drinking habits, taking the club with him down to the pits of debt and disrepute. There are continuous fights now between the two men.

Then one day the lawyer simply vanishes. Speculations are rife that he has been taken out by the husband of one of his many lovers. There are also speculations that his death is politically motivated. Straight after assuming control of the club he had been lured into one of the dominant political camps.

After a year, the lawyer's wife becomes the second wife of the bricklayer. The new family continues to build on the success of the soccer team. The young light-complexioned son of the bricklayer is the happiest in the current set-up. He is adored by both his biological mother and his adopted mother. His adopted mother can't stand the antics of her own swarthy biological son.

Sizwe was shivering by the time he tucked the manuscript under the mattress. 'When I was young, if I made soup and I was chopping...'

The following day, his mother left early for town to do some shopping.

'Your mother has left for town,' his father said. 'Quick, go and fetch your friend so I can give you the herb to cure you of your sickness.'

Dube knew his wife disapproved of his herbs. Besides, she would have a fit should she discover that her only son was in the grip of venereal disease. Dube wanted to do things the manly way; there were some things which men had to do behind the backs of their womenfolk. That's how he had been brought up; that's one of the few nuggets of advice he had bestowed upon his son: Do not allow your woman to know all your secrets. As soon as his wife had flung herself into the early morning breeze outside, Dube rushed to the back of his house where he kept a stash of barks and leaves which he ground and boiled for a variety of ailments.

He took a handful of the herbs and plunged them into a huge cauldron which he brought fast to the boil.

Sizwe eased himself carefully out of bed in order not to hurt his throbbing private parts. He put on his extra-baggy jeans – sans underpants – and tackies. The house reeked of menthol.

He left the house, walking slowly up the street, making sure his private parts dangled free, not rubbing against his pants. As he turned the corner, he stumbled upon two dogs stuck together. He wondered if dogs ever got venereal disease. If so, how did they communicate their discomfort to others? Did they have a dog doctor who prepared herbs for them? God's mysteries were a dime a dozen.

As he neared his friend's place he tried to walk like a normal person, wary not to attract Thulani's mother's attention to his weird stride. Thankfully, she wasn't home. He greeted his friend, and they ambled away from the house, trying very hard to move like normal boys. The dogs which Sizwe had encountered earlier were no longer humping each other. They growled at the boys as they approached. In no position to run away from the dogs, the boys had to take a detour, using back streets until they reached Sizwe's house.

When they got there, Sizwe's father had poured the menthol-smelling mixture into a basin. He told the boys to take it to the bathroom, where the ritual would take place.

'Take off your pants, you dirty rascals,' he said gruffly.

'Are we going to bath in this concoction, Dad?'

'Shut up and follow my instructions.'

He produced a rubber syringe, which he filled with the fluid.

'What amazes me is that you seem to have contracted the same disease at the same time. Have you been doing a streamline on the same woman?'

'What's a streamline, Mr Dube?' Thulani wanted to know.

'It's when one guy offers his woman to another man to sleep with. This often happens when the man is angry with his woman, and then runs a streamline on her by inviting as many men as possible to have sex with her as punishment. It's the dirtiest thing you can imagine. Only dogs are capable of doing such a thing. Decent self-respecting men don't do these things. Sheeeeit!'

The boys looked at each other.

'Now, back to my question: Are you boys in the habit of sleeping with the same girl? Sizwe, I am talking to you! Did you sleep with the same girl?'

'Yes, Daddy.'

Dube recoiled from his son's words as if they were a punch to his face.

'What in God's heaven is happening to our children? Why in the name of the great King Shaka did you run a streamline on a poor man's daughter?'

'It wasn't a streamline like you described it, Mr Dube. It was more like the girl like approached us like and, and, uhm, offered us, uhm...'

'Dogs! Filth! Whose sons are you?' he balled his hands into fists.

Sizwe blurted out: 'But Dad and Thulani's dad have done the same thing on Sis Lovey, and we know it.'

Again Dube recoiled, opened his mouth, closed it again. He was sweating feverishly. With his huge tummy jumping excitedly ahead of him, he rushed towards the door to check it was closed.

'Does your mother know about this? Have you said anything to her about this, Sizwe?'

'No, Dad.'

'Good, keep it that way. Now, pants off and let's get on with the job.'

The boys took off their pants and positioned themselves on the floor, their backsides pointing in the air.

Sizwe complained: 'But, Dad, all that we what is to bring an end to the bad discharge and the sores. Why do you have to give us an enema? Maybe you should be using an ointment of some sort around our private parts.'

'I'm the herbalist here. The dirt must be removed from the inside. Asses in the air, your dirty boys.'

The old man put his enema to work. For the next two days the boys had runny tummies. On the third day, the infection was over, the sores had healed, the smelly discharge gone.

'Nolitha must pay for this,' Thulani said as the two of them took a leak at the school toilets, for the first time in many days enjoying the process of emptying their bladders.

'Don't ever mention that name to me again.'

They were so engrossed in the liberating experience of urinating that they hadn't realised their friend Kokoroshe had joined them: 'What has Nolitha done now?'

They told him. He laughed long and hard. 'Ag, gents, I should have warned you. Been there, done that, and big brother the lawyer took me to a doctor.'

Seventeen
The Return of the Shepherd

The first Sunday the Reverend Tembe led his flock in a prayer since his return from his wayward ways, the church was packed. The elders had spun an elaborate yarn explaining the disappearance of their leader. On one of his visits to the frail members of the church, it was explained, he had been accosted and kidnapped by members of a radical political sect. Members of the sect had been unhappy about the fact that the priest had officiated at the funeral of the controversial Mvubu, self-appointed mayor of Siyajabula.

After his kidnapping, the Reverend Tembe had been kept prisoner by the radicals, who intended killing him and using his body parts as muti they would use to fortify themselves against their political enemies. It was believed that if you mixed human liver with some herbs and consumed this mash, you were automatically rendered invincible; that this concoction turned the enemy's bullets to water.

'The Lord works in mysterious ways,' Elder Mahlangu shouted at the congregation, his mouth foaming. 'The Lord opened the gates of the dungeon and allowed his son to walk free. It reminds me of those gates behind which Daniel had been languishing, hallelujah, don't we have a friend in Christ?'

'We have a great friend in Christ!' the congregation chorused enthusiastically.

On the strength of this story the faithful had come out in their numbers to see this holy man of God who had defied the evil forces and was back with them in the world of the living, gallantly spreading the word of God.

Fast-thinking members of the congregation had put together some money to buy a live sheep. The beast was slaughtered early in the morning before the church service started. While the singing was in progress inside, some industrious women were busy with the pots behind the church building. This was one of the biggest moments in the history of the parish: the return of their priest who had been abducted. They had to feast, to celebrate his return, to cleanse him of bad luck.

The singing was highly spirited, the clapping of hands energetic. This is what the Reverend Tembe enjoyed most about the manner in which the Anglicans conducted their services. Unlike the Catholics, who were staid in their singing, sounding like Europeans who have no sense of rhythm, the Anglicans were spirited, clapping their hands, jumping about in the aisles if the mood took them.

The service today was handled by the senior deacons while the priest sat on his throne, basking in the glory of his own return to the world of the living, listening to prayers of thanks being uttered by grateful members of the congregation.

'Without our holy father, our church was dying,' one congregant after the other stood up to testify.

'Our great reverend is a gift from above, a blessing from God, hallelujah!'

On and on, members of the congregation sang and testified. The sweet aroma of cooking meat filled the air, adding more merriment and energy to the proceedings.

Thulani was seated on one of the benches at the front, singing like everyone else but not with the same energy and verve as the rest of the congregation. His mother sitting next to him was visibly bubbly, singing until tears flowed from her eyes. The senior archdeacon who had visited the Tembe household to offer succour to the reverend's wife was also weeping visibly.

Sizwe, who was sitting with his father in the men's section of the church, kept stealing glances at his friend. Sizwe's father was not an habitual churchgoer. He had visited the holy building every now and then since becoming friends with the priest. Otherwise, while both his wife and son went to church, he would be found looking very deep into his beer glass on Sundays. But this was a special day, the day he had to come and give support to his friend.

For his part, Sizwe could see that his friend was unhappy, jittery and restless. It was amazing to both boys how the world of grown-ups operated. Most of the people gathered here knew that the whole thing was a charade; in fact they couldn't wait until the service was over so they could go and eat meat and then proceed to the streets and shebeens, where they would wag their tongues about the biggest charade they'd ever seen.

Everybody lowered their singing voices when they realised that the good-looking son of their leader, the lovely, outspoken Thulani who was a good preacher in his own right, was getting up from his seat.

He broke into a new song, which was immediately taken up by the worshippers.

As the song died down, Thulani started in a strong voice to tell the story of the prodigal son and how he had gone astray and was finally forgiven and feted by his father on his return. There were murmurs inside the church, people exchanging glances as if to ask if it was proper that a child should get up and tell such a story. But Thulani was not done yet. The story told, he led the congregation in song again. He seemed relaxed, his face full of serenity and bliss. When the song was over, he told the congregation that before descending from the stage, he would like to leave his father's people with a few words to ruminate on.

He quoted from the Bible. 'The words I will leave you with are from Hebrews 13, from verse one: Let brotherly love continue. Be not forgetful to entertain strangers: for thereby some have entertained angels unawares. Remember them that are in bonds, as bound with them; and them which suffer adversity, as being yourselves also in the body. Marriage is honourable in all, and the bed undefiled: but whoremongers and adulterers God will judge.'

The archdeacon, who had been sitting apprehensively in his

seat, bolted up to the stage and broke into song, the congregation joining him, drowning the young man completely.

Thulani calmly descended, headed for the door and walked home, where he buried his head in his pillow. Back at the church, the service didn't last long. The feast that had been prepared was demolished in haste, and people flowed into the streets, which were soon awash with the excitement of what had taken place at church.

'You see what I told you, Mrs Msimang, the feast was but a cover-up of what really happened to the reverend.'

'But the son couldn't keep hiding the truth.'

'Yes, tell the truth and shame the devil, that's our reverend's motto, and his son lived up to it.'

'But I still think he was put up to it by his mother, that snake of a woman who plays the saint. Such a man of goodness shouldn't have married her in the first place.'

'Yes, I think he was driven to sin by her doings.'

'How I wish the reverend could kick her out!'

'Hawu! My friend, do you want to be the reverend's wife now?'

They laughed.

Later that evening, a visibly tired Reverend Tembe summoned his wife and son to the lounge. Sombrely, he thanked his son for telling the truth about him. He told them the real truth of what had happened to him.

'My dear children in the Lord,' he said to them, 'neither of you has faulted me. You have been good and loyal to me, both of you, and the girls at boarding school. But I have been communing with my conscience and have come to the conclusion that I am not worthy of your forgiveness. I have done you so much embarrassment and shame.'

'But, Daddy, we thank God that you are back,' his wife said, tears flowing from her eyes. 'We forgive you and welcome you back.'

'Mama, I don't think Daddy is finished.'

Behind a veil of tears, she scowled at her son.

'My son is right. I see a lot of me in this son of mine, forthright, not afraid. But yes, I am not finished. I have been thinking and praying, my children. I have realised that not only am I not worthy of your forgiveness, but I am also not worthy of your company. You see, I realised some time ago that I had strayed from the path the Lord had chosen for me. I tried to get married, start a family, settle down. That's not my destiny, I have since realised. I have been living a lie all along. It's time to face the truth, to stare my destiny in the eye, for I cannot change God's will. I am going to take leave of you, my children. I need to be on my own. You will be taken care of financially, but I can't bear living with you any more. The outstanding balance will be taken care of, and I will contribute towards your monthly bills. A friend of mine has offered me a post as a private teacher at one of the schools. I am done with the Church.'

Thulani did not hear the rest of it. He left the room, went out of the gate and started walking aimlessly, not in the direction of his friend's house.

Sobbing bitterly, Mrs Tembe coaxed her husband to their bedroom. 'You can't leave us just like that. You can't leave us. We have done nothing wrong to you. We truly forgive you. Come on, kiss me, make love to me if that's enough proof that I have forgiven you, that I still love you.'

But the reverend was unrepentant. He left the house the following day.

Later that afternoon, Mrs Tembe vented her frustration on her son: 'You chased my husband away with your evil tongue.'

'You have always told me that the truth will liberate us, that we should tell the truth and shame the devil. And that's exactly what I wanted to do. In fact everyone in that church already knew the truth. They were laughing behind our backs at the charade we put up. All I did was reassure them that we all knew the truth, and it wasn't hidden.'

She stormed out of the kitchen, went to her bedroom where she locked herself in for the next two days. She called in sick at the furniture shop where she worked. They not only gave her the time off on full pay; they said they understood.

Eighteen
Mr Enterprice

'A person doesn't need to wonder what your calling in life is, Mr Dube,' a tall thin man was saying jocularly to Dube. 'Even as I hand you the keys to your new shop I can tell that you are a born entrepreneur. Even your build, your persona, betrays you as a businessman.'

Dube laughed heek-heek-heek, his tummy moving rhythmically to the noises he was making, 'Thank you very much, my dear sir, I will take care of your good shop.'

'It's no longer mine. It's yours now. You've paid me my money, and all I can do now is wish you well on your future.'

Over the past few years, the soccer team that Dube had been running with his friend the reverend had performed so well it won a number of sponsorships. With its high profile in the media, it won the attention of the bigger teams in Johannesburg, who came running to snap up the promising young players who had been groomed by the duo. As a result, the team had become a financially viable entity. But with his friend gone, Dube realised he wouldn't be able to cope with the running of the club. He quit it and reverted to his old hobby – horse racing – which he had pursued fervently as a young man.

Week after week, he played. Sometimes he won, most times he lost. Six months after his religious engagement with his old hobby, he hit the jackpot. He won forty thousand rands, a princely sum of money at the time. The entrepreneur in him got thinking.

He took over a faltering corner café in the neighbourhood, with a view to turning it into a supermarket. His wife was excited: 'At last you're going to be running a real business now, my dear Dube.

Not those noisy smelly ducks you used to sell.'

Father, mother and son got down to business, cleaning the new premises. Within a week, shopfitters had finished installing shelves. The cash register company paid a number of visits to ensure that the machines had been properly installed. A sign writer was commissioned to design a huge billboard for the face of the new supermarket. He delivered it promptly as per specification, in red, yellow and green colours, with the words MR ENTERPRICE.

The Dubes stood in front of their new shop, beaming at the billboard. But then Mrs Dube the teacher noticed the mistake: 'It should be Mr Enterprise. E-N-T-E-R-P-R-I-S-E.'

Sizwe agreed, but decided to say instead: 'No, Mama, you see, what Papa and I were trying to get to when we commissioned this work of art was that the customer will ENTER our premises, and we will give her a good PRICE. See?'

He winked at his parents. Dube massaged his tummy, and went heek-heek-heek-heek!

Even before the shop opened for business, Sizwe enlisted the help of his friends Thulani and Kokoroshe, who helped him offload things from delivery trucks, count the stock and ensure that the shelves were properly packed. Fulltime staff were also hired. The supermarket opened for trading on October 10, 1990. Thulani and Kokoroshe were happy to earn extra bucks on Friday afternoons and at weekends. But Kokoroshe had to shuttle between this shop and his own mother's Paradise Road. The attraction held by Mr Enterprice was that he earned real money based on duties performed, whereas at home he was paid in kind.

As soon as the trading stabilised, Mr Dube told his son to go back home so he could concentrate on his books. Dube and his servants were competent enough to take care of the shop.

'But, Dad, I like it here at the shop. I can concentrate on my books while looking after the shop as well.'

What he enjoyed about the shop, a fact he didn't mention to his father, was that the girls beamed at him as he sat behind the counter. After all these years of being shunned by one and all, he was now Mr Somebody. Mr Enterprise!

But in addition to watching the endless parade of girls who were at pains to get his eye and admiration, he found that he enjoyed the endless sound of voices. For a long time he had been confined in his bedroom, nose buried in his books. Now he could watch people choose their foodstuffs, listen to husbands and wives arguing about their families' priorities. From these observations he had started writing stories he could read aloud to his parents and elicit some laughs.

'We better watch our mouths, sweetheart,' his mother said as they watched TV one night. 'Mr Writer here is watching our every move, recording our utterances.'

With the exams looming on the horizon, Sizwe had no choice but to stay away from the shop and concentrate on his books. His mother became a constant presence at the shop as soon as she knocked off from work at school. The Dubes had planned everything properly and didn't think it was prudent for her to quit teaching right now. Dube had brought trusted relatives from both sides of the family to help run the shop while he drove in and out of Exclusive Park in his new bakkie, taking care of the strategic side of business.

'Now, my dear boy,' Dube told his son one day, 'the business is doing so well you don't have to worry about university fees.'

Sizwe beamed proudly as his father droned on about other plans he had for his thriving business. All that was important to him was that he would be going to university. He couldn't wait.

Nineteen
Like Father, Like Son

The Standard Nines were hurtling towards exam time. But before the exams proper they had to go through what was known as Revision Time. This was a period of about two weeks during which both teachers and pupils suddenly woke up from the long slumber of indifference and laziness to the realisation that the exams were just around the corner and serious work couldn't be postponed any more.

Panic set in. Nerves were on edge. Teachers, many of whom had during the course of the year spent endless hours at local shebeens or holed up in the staffroom working on their own private studies so they could earn more academic credits, suddenly remembered that they were here at the school to do the job of getting the darn kids to the next grade. Now, during Revision Time, the teachers became pests swarming around the panicky pupils, harassing them with questions: Have you decided what you want to study after finishing high school? Have you started applying for bursaries and scholarships for university?

The pupils had spent four years in high school already, but nobody had bothered to think about career guidance all along. Now, with just one year to go, they had to have answers on what they wanted to do after high school and where they were going to get funds for tertiary education. In addition to responding about their future careers, they had to be ready for the exams. In order to make sure their pupils were ready for the exams, the teachers moved about their classes wielding canes. Canes were good for helping pupils remember the answers to questions about grammar, the Pythagoras theorem, algebra, and other items of information which, to some pupils around this time, sounded new and fresh from the shelves of academia.

It never seemed to strike the teachers that, had they started working with their children with such fervour right from the beginning of the year, the kids would pass with flying colours; the teachers would be praised for good work; the Minister of Education could report to the nation that the country was turning the corner in terms of producing children who would ensure that South Africa became a winning nation. Everybody would be happy.

The fact that the teachers remembered their responsibilities so late in the year engendered panic. Girls succumbed to mass hysteria, with frequent scenes being recorded of three or four girls suddenly breaking into long anguished screams in class. Zulu traditional healers who had to be called in during these trying times did not interpret these screaming explosions like westerners, who believed these were a result of undue pressure and panic. The traditional healers gave the poor girls herbs and enemas to calm them down. Their explanation was simply that the girls had been bewitched by jealous enemies who did not want them to write their exams so they could proceed to the next grade, the final grade in high school.

It was in this crucible of panic and excitement that Thulani and Sizwe found themselves towards the end of October 1990. The two were bright and diligent students all right, but the terror of the time did not leave them unscathed.

On Friday their Afrikaans teacher, a light-skinned, bearded fellow with the surname of Mhlophe, was taking them through their paces in Afrikaans grammar, checking if they still remembered the future perfect tense, future tense, and so on.

Mhlophe was so fervent about getting the right answers from his pupils that he was foaming at the mouth. He jumped from the top of one desk to the next, hurling a question at a pupil, getting the wrong answer, and lashing the hapless kid with his cane across the shoulders. Even Sizwe, usually calm, collected and confident, was getting his tenses mixed up as a result.

Every time the teacher reached Thulani's desk, the boy had a ready smile and the correct answer. Sinking into a demented state, the teacher suddenly started lashing at him. 'You know all the damn answers, so why couldn't you share your wisdom with your classmates!' On and on, he lashed across the boys' shoulders, across his back, on his arms when the young man tried to parry the blows.

'Ag, voetsek, man. I've had enough of your shit!' Thulani heard himself saying.

The teacher recoiled in horror. He seemed to have woken up from a trance.

'Tell me if you want to kill me, and let's get out of this class and get things settled like men out in the street!' With those words, Thulani, his shirt sleeves torn and bloody, gathered his books and left the class. Sizwe fumbled with his own books, stood up, but sat down again. Kokoroshe did not hesitate; he took his books and followed behind his friend.

The teacher walked, like one in a trance, out of the classroom, to the staffroom. From there he gathered his books and left.

It was much later in the evening, staggering from one of the low-class shebeens, that the teacher was accosted by two figures. One of the two had something that looked like a bottle in his left hand. He seemed to be taking a gulp from the bottle, but he suddenly spat whatever he had been drinking, into the teacher's face, at the same time flicking a match.

The teacher was engulfed in a ball of fire, sustaining serious burns. He quit teaching. Thulani left town.

As for Kokoroshe, as soon as his mother heard what had taken place at school, she was livid, punching him as she had pummelled other men in her previous life.

'I will not have an uneducated son here,' she had said finally, and personally drove him back to school.

The principal was highly apologetic. Kokoroshe wrote his exam, but even as he did so, he wondered why.

Twenty
Heat

Durban summers are searing, humid and sticky. Breathing is like drowning in a cauldron filled with boiling water. Birds sometimes faint in mid-flight. Ants that accidentally venture out of their holes are fried into nothingness within an instant. Dogs lie in the sand, tongues hanging out, sometimes never to rise again. Rock rabbits emerge from hide-outs in rock crevices, panting for breath. Flies disappear to wherever flies come from in the first place. On these sweltering days, those who have access to water can be forgiven for taking at least three cold showers a day, to keep cool and chase away body odours. Zulus in this hot city have an expression for this scorching weather: It's so hot the fish are running away from the river.

It was during one of these sweltering Friday afternoons that Mrs Tembe sat on her porch, sweating and thinking. Her husband had left, and her son had followed soon after. Now she had to face this house alone, she had to face life alone. For days on end she had cried, unable to think beyond her current reality. She walked about in a haze, unable to see things around her, the world having become a vortex in which she spun around helplessly.

The Church authorities had installed a new priest in her church. As a result she had lost her status, her privileges, such as they were. Luckily the house she lived in had been paid off by her husband, so she didn't have to worry about being kicked out. He had worked on a freelance basis as a translator for a Christian publishing house. Also, the priest her husband was living up to his word; every month he deposited into her bank account a stipend that made her life bearable. Yet all these things did not ameliorate her emotional anguish. She longed for the lost comfort of having a husband and a son around the house. These had been the pillars of her strength.

When her two daughters who stayed at boarding school during the year came back home, she decided to send them to her own mother; she couldn't bear the sight of them being saddened by her current state.

Tears started falling down her cheeks as she remembered the days they'd spent together visiting the beach, looking holy and important as they attended Church jamborees and functions, travelling overseas on Church business, being entertained by important white members of the Church at their sumptuous houses in the great suburbs of the north of Johannesburg.

All that was gone now, all because of a harlot by the name of Lovey. What kind of name was that in any case? What puzzled her, however, was that the same Lovey who had broken her marriage had not followed Tembe to wherever he had disappeared to. The same Lovey was busy using her mother's den of iniquity as a launching pad for raids on other people's marriages. Why had Lovey not followed her husband?

The more she thought about the two men in her life, the more she realised that they had never really been a part of her. True, she had been married to Tembe for almost twenty years. True, she had given birth to her brat of a son. She suddenly realised that the two men had been physical presences for her, around the house. But they had never insinuated themselves into the depth of her emotions.

It was now December, almost two months had passed since the son left, the father having gone a few weeks before. But she found she was coping without them, although there were bouts of sadness and tears now and then. She was shocked by the sudden realisation, because she had never imagined her life without her husband.

For this newly discovered peace of mind that was gradually taking possession of her she thanked her friend Mrs Dube, who sat with her patiently and spoke to her about men, about matters of the heart. 'All you have to focus on right now is raising your kids, making sure they finish school and proceed to pursue careers of their choice,' Mrs Dube had said. 'Your focus on something close to your heart will bring back the equilibrium that you require to cope with the stresses and the challenges of life.'

Guided by Mrs Dube's observations, she had decided that her daughters would not be going back to boarding school the following year. After all, taking them there had been their father's idea; he had thought the townships, with their wide-eyed boys, were no places for girls. They had to be confined at seminaries under the watchful gaze of nuns. Now she had decided to bring them back close to her, to savour their company, to nurture a tighter bond with them. After all, she was their mother.

She looked at her watch: five thirty.

She walked inside the house and dialled the Dubes' number.

'Hello?' It was Sizwe's voice.

'Hello, boy, is Mommy around?'

'No, she's gone to some meeting. She'll be coming home around seven.'

'What are you doing sitting at home instead of helping your poor daddy at the shop?'

'He chased me away. Said whenever I am around there's a flock of girls milling around the shop, not buying anything but creating unnecessary disorder.'

They laughed over that one.

She said, 'By the way, your friend left a boxful of books and notebooks here. He wrote me a letter the other day to say you must come and collect them and do whatever you please with them.'

After a moment's hesitation, Sizwe said, 'I'll be coming over in the next ten minutes, aunty.'

'See you then, son.'

Sizwe had always thought he was a more diligent writer than his friend Thulani. He conceded that his friend was more imaginative, but he always seemed distracted, and playful to the point of losing focus on the dream he had always held in his heart of hearts: to become a writer. But when he saw notebook upon notebook, typescripts and sketches, Sizwe realised that his friend had been working hard but quietly in the privacy of his room.

Even though he was busy poring on the notebooks, his eyes couldn't help stealing glances at his friend's mother. He had been sceptical about coming over to the house because he hated to be close to sadness and grief. But far from looking depressed, the old lady was cheerful, radiant even. The minute the word 'radiant' registered in his mind, he paused, stole a glance at her. She was concentrating on some photo in Thulani's album. As a result he had enough time to look at her.

Unlike in the past when she used to cover her head with a doek, a chiffon or some other head gear, she wore nothing over her head now, her hair done in a fashionable greasy perm which went well with her very light complexion. Ha! She was wearing lipstick. Where she used to wear long flowing dresses, today she had on a white blouse and a skirt that reached just above her knees, liberating the rest of her legs to show themselves to the world. The white blouse she had on was open at the neck, showing her very light-skinned cleavage.

He looked away, embarrassed.

Suddenly he started sobbing, surprised that he had been holding such a reservoir of emotions inside his body. He was looking at a picture of himself and Thulani standing on the edge of a swimming pool, ready to take the plunge into the blue water.

His friend's mother looked up from the photo album she'd been scrutinising. She crossed the floor, gave him a hug, clucking her tongue sadly. He inhaled the fragrance of her body.

He deliberately dropped the picture to the floor so that he could break the embrace. He proceeded towards other books, pausing every now and then to admire a sparkling phrase in one short story or the other. For the next hour they went through the collection of documents, making nostalgic comments. At some stage, when her back was turned on him, she bent forward to reach for yet another photo album. In that fraction of a minute, he saw the line of her panties under her skirt. He felt his heart throbbing in his ears. He looked away quickly.

'Aunty,' he said, 'I'll take one of the boxes today, and come back for more tomorrow.'

'That's fine by me, as long as you take all of them away from here as soon as possible. I can't bear the sight of them. They remind me so much of him I want to cry.'

'I'll go through them, and choose what I like.'

'No, take everything. He said in his letter you should take everything. He doesn't care what you do with his make-believe stories, as long as you take them. He trusts your intellect. He says you might want to correct them, polish them up a bit and have them published. However, he says when you do get them published, do not use his name. He's given me a name – what do you call it? a pseudonymn – that he would like to use.'

She handed him a typed sheaf of manuscript. It was a short story with the title 'Ramu the Hermit', 'written by Vusi Mntungwa'.

'Here, take this letter from him which gives you the lowdown on what you can and can't do with the stories.'

'Thank you, aunty, see you tomorrow then.'

'Goodbye, say hi to your mom. I'll probably see her tomorrow as well.'

As he left the house, a familiar phrase bubbled to the surface of his mind: 'When I was young, if I made soup and I was chopping onions ...' The phrase lingered in the air, unfinished, tantalising, a whiff of what makes women lovely everywhere.

Twenty-One
Ramu the Hermit

For the next two days, Sizwe locked himself in his room and savoured the literary treasure trove his friend had left behind. He wondered where he'd gone to, what he would do for a living seeing that he hadn't finished even his high school.

He comforted himself by thinking that the hardships of the world would bring Thulani back to his senses, back to his mother's bosom. That way he would have learned his lesson. He had read the letter explaining exactly what he had to do with the rough drafts and notes. He was at liberty to correct the notes, package them into intelligible stories, and send them to the many literary journals for publication. The only proviso was that they should not be published under Thulani Tembe's name, but under Vusi Mntungwa's.

> I am not proud of the stories I produced, and would therefore be loath to having them published under my name. I am still in the early stages of the great discipline of writing. I do not want to be as presumptuous as to think I am worthy of having my name used alongside any printed material. Maybe the time will come when I will feel confident enough for this. So far, do as you please with these notes and drafts. I can't tell you where I have gone to, or what I intend doing when I get there. I suppose I am entering that process of finding myself. Maybe I will never find myself at all. Who am I anyway to presume there's a possibility, whatsoever, of finding my own self?

There were many other notes, beginnings of essays, unfinished plays and so on. There was even an unfinished novel. But try as he might, Sizwe's eyes kept going back to 'Ramu the Hermit'. So he sat comfortably and started reading it:

Ramu the Hermit
by Vusi Mntungwa

Ramu sat cross-legged in a meditative posture, his head held high in the air and his eyes glued to the heavily curtained window. For a moment his mind's eye rejoiced in the sight of a battalion of bejewelled Hindu deities, their foreheads resplendent with sacred ash and their bangles tinkling with every move they made. He saw a serpent, the holy serpent of Lord Shiva. It stood on its tail and swayed sideways to the music of the tablas and tambourines. The all-seeing Lord Krishna with his multiple hands sat serenely atop a chariot.

Suddenly Ramu's thread of communication with his gods was cut short, disturbed by the high-pitched voice of the muezzin calling from the mosque opposite his house. It was Friday afternoon and the Muslims were engrossed in prayer. The unsynchronised cries of 'Allah uAkbar' pierced the air outside and filtered through the seams of Ramu's tightly closed windows.

And at the same time, in wavy ripples of sound, the up-tempo music drifted from the house next door into Ramu's room of prayer. He cursed the earth and asked God why he tolerated the existence of such noisy people, people who disturbed him in prayer; people who didn't have any sense of decency; people who didn't have respect for other people's gods; people who were forever invading his privacy and making it impossible for him to communicate with his gods.

In his mind he tried to reconstruct the Divine Lord Krishna and his entourage, to no avail. Voices from the mosque rose and fell; the music from next door gained momentum. It was Friday, after all, a time when mere mortals like the people next door were beginning their orgy of noise, drunkenness and – oh, how could he allow his mind to be contaminated by the mere thought of the woman next door and her stream of male visitors?

He had chosen his way. The holy way. The only way to heaven. The only gate to eternal happiness. He was not going to be moved.

'To hell with the devil,' Ramu muttered under his breath and tried to marshal his thoughts away from the filth surrounding him. He made a mental note to start looking for a better place elsewhere, in a quieter, more civilised neighbourhood. He wished Kali, the goddess of death, could at that very instant come and wipe out all the sluts like the woman next door, bitches who had reduced their bodies – God's temples – into mere mattresses for all men to loll on indiscriminately for a price. Their bodies were now waste bins in which every man emptied his tank of unwanted garbage. He had read of the wrath of Kali. He shuddered slightly when the goddess's sword took shape in his mind.

The number of bitches is definitely on the increase, he mused.

Why was he allowing his mind to flirt with such earthly, if not evil, thoughts? he asked himself. Was he not on the threshold of being a sanyasi, an ascetic whose life is devoted to the worship of the All-Wise, the Almighty?

His swami had taught him to chant the holy mantra in order to purge his mind of dirty thoughts. He started intoning: 'Hare Krishna, Hare Krishna, Hare Rama, Hare Rama, Krishna Krishna, Rama Rama...'

He chanted for hours, but as soon as he paused, worldly thoughts assailed his mind. How proud he was that he would be the first African sanyasi in the whole of Chatsworth township, a residential area inhabited by people of Indian extraction. Because of the country's apartheid and segregation laws, few Africans – or blacks – lived here. They were descendants of Zanzibaris who had been brought to Durban at the turn of the nineteenth century to work in white people's sugar cane plantations because the locals, proud and pig-headed as they were, had refused to work for foreigners in their own native land. Except for their skin colour, the new arrivals had nothing in common with the local blacks. They spoke Zanzibari and Swahili, while the local blacks spoke Zulu, Xhosa, Sotho and other indigenous southern African tongues. The Zanzibaris were of the Muslim faith.

Like the Zanzibaris, Ramu had been brought up under strict Muslim conditions. But now that he was twenty-four, he thought he was old enough to make his own decisions about the life he wanted to lead. So, he had not long ago 'defected', as his detractors said, to the Hare Krishna, a sect of the broader Hindu faith.

'Inshallah,' the cry strayed from the mosque, startling Ramu back into reality. The music continued to play at the house next door, more vigorously now.

I should have gone to the temple where there is no noise, Ramu thought to himself. But again, his swami had insisted that he keep away from the temple these days. He should stay indoors by himself so that he could learn self-discipline, restraint. His tenacity was on test.

Was he failing the test? What else could he do to rechannel his thoughts to the Almighty?

Impulsively, he paged through the Bhagavad Gita which had been resting in front of him. He scanned it carelessly and closed it again. He carefully put it in front of him and broke into a sastra, a Vedic hymn, in an attempt to chase evil thoughts away from his room of prayer.

Within an instant he became so absorbed in the hymn that he did not feel the numbness of his buttocks resulting from his hours of sitting in the otherwise uncomfortable lotus position on the bare floor. With his mind's eye he saw himself in the midst of devotees in saffron robes dancing gaily as they rhythmically clashed their cymbals. Others were beating their hand drums and singing their hearts out in praise of Lord Krishna.

He was so meditative that he could feel the blood coursing in his veins. He could feel it curdle with the ecstasy of spiritual rediscovery.

And then, as if in a dream, he heard a crackling sound echoing in his ears. Slowly, he was roused from his trance. He realised that he wasn't dreaming after all; there were screams and a jangle of rat-a-tat sounds outside. He jumped to his feet and peeped through his thick curtains.

But he couldn't see anything out there in the street. Cursing, he thought he might have been in holy dreamland. He closed the curtain and went to the picture of Lord Krishna which was hanging from a wall and gave a slight bow before resuming his position on the floor. He tried to reconstruct his link with the spiritual world again. No sooner had he started chanting the mantra than he was jolted back to reality by the crash of his window and a missile missing him by inches. Evil spirits! Alarmed, he looked at the missile – a stone – which had fallen in a corner near his small table that was nearly invisible under the volumes of Sanskrit literature.

Nervously, he parted the curtains and peeped into the street, now enveloped in smoke and sound. Ah, he had smelt this before. Teargas! What was happening? Fiddling with his dhoti and slipping his feet into his sandals, he dashed for the door.

Once in the street, he saw it all: youths, each with his face masked with a towel, were stoning an armoured police vehicle. The police, some of them on top of the vehicle and others scattered all over the street, were systematically shooting at the youngsters. Why? Why on this street? Still dazed, confused, Ramu felt something sting him on his bare left shoulder.

'Run, comrade! Don't let them catch you!'

'Run for cover, my man!'

'Gooi the guava juice, my bra!'

At this, there was a booming sound as a small boy threw the guava juice – a petrol bomb – at the police. When it hit the front of the vehicle, it exploded in flames.

"Ouch! The swine got me in the thigh,' someone cried.

Police guns continued to belch fire.

The praying and singing had long stopped at the mosque. So had the music at Ramu's neighbour's.

Grimacing from the pain locked in his left biceps, Ramu dashed for safety. His dhoti billowed as he fled. He jumped over the fence into a yard at the back of his house. He crouched near a bush of tall dahlias. He hated the nauseating smell of these flowers but could not run any further, having seen another police vehicle parked in the street he'd been running to. He knew it would be unsafe to go and lock himself up in his house. The police could just go straight in there and haul him out. They were ruthless. The State of Emergency gave them powers to arrest people without a warrant and detain them indefinitely, without charging them.

Panting and his chest heaving, dazed from the effects of the teargas, he touched the spot where the stray rubber bullet had caught him. The pain burnt and seemed to pierce the depths of his being. He was not bleeding profusely but he felt as if the pain could kill him. Never in his life had he felt so much searing distress from such a small wound. Now he felt dizzy, weak. Rubber bullet wounds could be fatal, he'd been told.

The hullabaloo in the street had not subsided; the police vehicles were now racing up and down in pursuit of stone-throwing youths. The sound of the engines of the police vehicles was accompanied by the staccato sound of shooting. There were cries of agony.

He must have fallen unconscious for, when he next came to his senses, he was in a strange place. Flicking his eyes open nervously, he looked around. Ha! He was in the bed of his neighbour, the woman who was every man's pillow.

Rage welled in his heart. He sweated profusely. His heart pounded as if it wanted to knock its way out of his chest. He tried to prop himself up from the bed but he was too weak. Within an instant the woman appeared from the kitchen with a tray bearing an orange, a banana and a glass of Coke.

She put the tray on a dressing table and loomed in the doorway, smiling. She leapt forward when she realised that the patient was again trying to get up.

'No, don't do that. You're hurting yourself. You're too weak. I think you bled a lot. But I couldn't take you to the clinic. The police were waiting at the entrance for people with gunshot wounds.'

'Weak? Who's weak? What am I doing here anyway?' He struggled to get up but his body wouldn't carry him.

'Look at what time it is now. It's way past midnight. Have some fruit and go to sleep. You should rest. I'll explain everything to you in the morning when you've had enough time to rest.'

'No... you... you... tell me now what happened! You witch. You sorceress. You slut. Have you bewitched me into coming into your bed like the rest of your men? Men who waste their holy seed on you?'

She merely smiled and smoothed the duvet over him. He realised with shock that he was naked.

He smelled of a strange perfume, he realised.

'What have you done to me? How did I get here? Tell me before I set the wrath of my god upon you,' he said, pointing an accusing finger at her.

'Okay,' she put in, 'let me explain before you get too angry with me. I was running away from the police when I stumbled upon you. You were lying unconscious near a bush.'

He groaned.

'As soon as I recognised your face I said to myself, "I can't let the holy man die out here in the wilderness." I decided to hide myself until the police had gone away so that I could take you home and nurse your wound.'

'You stinking daughter of the devil!'

'Wait, let me explain. I haven't done anything wrong. As a former nurse I know how to treat severe bruises. I also know that inhaling teargas can complicate some people's respiratory system. So I was merely helping you.'

He concentrated hard on her.

'As soon as the police vacated the area, I dragged you into the house so that I could help you.'

The wall-clock in an adjoining room chimed one o'clock.

She smiled. For the first time he noticed that she wore a transparent nightie which showed the better part of her thighs. At the joining of her thighs was a dark mound of flesh.

She was watching his eyes. She said: 'I think it's time for both of us to sleep. It's late.'

As an afterthought she added, 'But first, have some cold drink and fruit.'

She roamed around the foot of the bed near the oak dressing table, which was laden with perfume bottles, an array of cream containers, combs of all shapes and sizes, and the unmentionable paraphernalia of her class, style, taste, trade.

Ramu's temples were pounding steadily now. What would his swami say should he find him in the company of a woman notorious for her loose morals, a self-confessed, self-advertising, self-praising prostitute? What was the all-seeing Lord Krishna saying at this very moment?

His throat was suddenly parched. He looked at her fixedly. Her stomach was a large blob of fat and her arms were as fleshy as huge bananas. Her big breasts heaved rhythmically when she laughed – which she did a lot. Her buttocks were like a giant pumpkin and they danced like jelly when she moved.

He asked himself what pleasure men derived from such an obnoxious-looking creature. He wanted to know why so many men paid their hard-earned money to loll on those rubbery arms. He couldn't understand why men risked breaking their marriages just because of this slut who belonged to the eternal inferno of hell.

His train of thought was brought to a standstill by the woman when she slid into the warmth of the duvet cover beside him. He shifted towards the wall, avoiding the slightest contact with her.

She drew closer to him. He moved. The bed was too small for both of them to sleep comfortably. They had to huddle together, somewhat. Or else one of them had to sleep on the floor, or sleep on one of the rickety sofas in the living room.

Neither of them uttered a word. The main light had been turned off. The bedside lamp burned dimly, lending what seemed to be a touch of romance to this rather tense atmosphere. Still shifting uneasily, she paged through an old copy of a girlie magazine. He couldn't help catching a glimpse of a naked woman posing in positions he'd never imagined possible.

'Let us sleep,' she said, sighing. She put the magazine on the bedside table and sank into the warmth of the bed.

Ramu's anger had transformed itself into inexplicable helplessness. His coldness had been thawed by the warmth of the human mass next to him. He was sweating now. His lips quivered, but words refused him. He could feel the blood coursing through every vein in his body. Now and then his body trembled. His hair seemed to stand on end. His ears burned. A wave of sensation shot from his head and raced down his spinal cord.

His long-suppressed desire whirled around his groin and exploded out of his penis in torrents, like preserved oil from a burst pipe.

The sheets were flooded by the deluge of wasted human seed. The woman tittered, feeling the warm oil bathe her thighs. Ramu grabbed her impulsively, and let out a deep sigh.

'I'll have my cold drink and fruit now,' he croaked.
END.

Like the character in the story, Sizwe threw his head back and sighed. His hands were trembling. What was the story about? Had Thulani decided to join the Hare Krishnas as a holy man? No matter how he looked at it, this was a powerful story. He couldn't subtract or add anything to it. Damn! How had Thulani imagined such a story?

No, he had stolen it. Yes, that could be the only explanation. That could also explain why he was reluctant to attach his own name to it. A sigh of relief escaped his lips again. He decided there and then to send the story as it was to one of the literary magazines. Surely the rightful owner of the story would raise a storm at this blatant instance of plagiarism.

Aha! That's what you do to thieves, Sizwe cackled.

The tantalising phrase came to his mind again: 'When I was young, if I made soup and I was chopping...'

Twenty-Two
Nightmares

Sizwe's mind was in a haze in 1991 when he entered his final year of high school. Never before had he had to grapple with so many issues, issues which jostled for his immediate attention and action. For one, he had resuscitated his relationship with Nolitha. He'd encouraged her to see a doctor about her condition, which she had readily done. They enjoyed a healthy sexual relationship now. She seemed to have mended her ways, not succumbing to the whims of her body at the appearance of just any boy. With his newfound wealth, he could afford to take her to town and spend long hours at the bigger nightclubs there whenever she was off for the weekend from Paradise Road.

He had to keep his eyes wide open, for there were many vultures intent on pouncing on beautiful girls like Nolitha. That Nolitha had not progressed much at school sometimes bothered him. But then he took solace in the fact that she was only a temporary girlfriend, a crutch that would help him to leap into the big league. By the time he got to university, he told himself, he would have learned enough from Nolitha to be able to navigate the turbulent waters of falling in and out of love all by himself.

But still, he couldn't help panicking, finding himself appealing to Nolitha: 'Sweetie pie, walking about in such an industrialised nation as ours without education is calling for trouble. You must try to quit your job and go back to school.'

'How many times will I have to tell you I don't have the money to go back to school? You've seen the shack, the home that I live in. Do you think I am proud of living in that hovel? I am not. I just don't have the means. You are lucky to have parents who are educated and rich, I don't have any parents to speak of.'

These talks always ended inconclusively, with Nolitha putting in at last, 'But with a clever and educated husband like you, I have no reason to worry. You will work hard, bring the money home, and I will bear you beautiful kids.'

Much as they loved going to the bigger nightclubs in town, their final loyalty still lay with Paradise Road, where they spent time with Kokoroshe. Both boys had started drinking harder than before. And, of all people, it was Sizwe who had introduced Kokoroshe to dagga-smoking. The latter had in the past observed boys his age smoking dagga inside the toilets at school. He, however, had thus far given the herb a wide berth. But now that the boys were seniors at high school, they thought it was only proper that they should start preparing themselves for university, the grown-up world out there.

Another thing that had suddenly seized Sizwe's attention was that he was having more fights with his father. These revolved around the boy's increasingly public drinking sprees. But they also related to the fact that ever since he had become something of a local celebrity with the opening of his new shop, his father had started, with renewed vigour, chasing after women. Most disgustingly, he wasn't hiding his sexual appetite any more, stopping his car in the middle of the street to accost a good-looking woman passing by – or so the ubiquitous storytellers said.

'Dad, I think it's time we spoke about these things, man to man,' Sizwe confronted his father one Friday, his body pounding with four beers' worth of courage. Sizwe had just come home, finding his father alone, drinking beer and watching TV. 'Ever since you opened the supermarket, you seem to have become popular with the women.'

'I don't discuss these things with kids.'

'But people are talking, Dad. They say you've been seen at such and such places with Sis Lovey. Shame on you, Daddy. You know what Lovey did to your friend, what she did to his marriage.'

'I am warning you, boy,' he said, getting up from his chair, his tummy wiggling this and that way as he pointed an accusing finger at his son. 'I've been drinking alcohol all my life, well, almost, but I don't ever remember being abusive to my elders just because of booze.'

'Okay,' Sizwe said, lowering his voice in defeat, 'I won't say any more. But Mama will get to hear of this.'

He shouldn't have said that. The big man lunged at him, banging a hard right punch into the middle of the boy's tummy. The boy gasped, bent forward, and started vomiting.

'But my mama will still get to hear about this.'

His father connected his huge open palm across the boy's face. His nose started bleeding.

Sizwe was shocked. His father had never been so violent to him before. He had whipped him when he was still a kid, yes, but doing all this with love and a sense of caring; today he was violent.

The father helped his son to his feet, took him to the toilet where he cleaned him. He went back to the lounge and mopped up the vomit.

Sizwe had just emerged from the bathroom, still dabbing his red nose with a towel when the door went open and his mother walked in.

'What happened to you? Where is this blood from?'

'Ag,' Dube said casually, 'the boy was attacked by some thugs in the street. Tell her what happened.'

'I was just turning the corner, when bam! A punch exploded on my left cheek. And they were all over my pockets, luckily I didn't have much money.'

'Shame,' she said, 'poor thing, they thought you had on you some takings from the shop. Come, let Mama see what they did to you.'

This was just one of many of his violent encounters with his father. He conceded that he had not been tactful enough, but the older man was also losing the respect of his family by flirting with women in public.

Above all this, however, what troubled his mind most were the discoveries he had made from the manuscripts left to him by his friend Thulani. If he were to be honest with himself, in the depth of his heart of hearts he had hoped that, by deciding to disappear, his friend had done him a favour. He would no longer be there to remind him of his own intellectual inferiority, of his limited writing capabilities. But the stories were going to be a permanent reminder to him. No matter which way he looked at things, their fates were interlinked.

It had been two months since the story called 'Ramu the Hermit' had been published in one of the journals. No one had come forth to claim it as his own. This bothered Sizwe, for it proved what he had feared: that the story was indeed the work of his own friend. It bothered him even more that he shouldn't be celebrating, congratulating his friend for a job well done. He felt a constriction around his heart whenever he read Thulani's pieces. How could one so young express himself so flawlessly? Sizwe himself had read extensively and had been practising his art for a long time, but he could only gape at the sparkling prose of his friend's, the clarity of thought, the economy of words.

Of late he had started having nightmares. In one of them he saw himself being chased by a group of Zulu warriors dressed in animal skins. One of them had the face of his own friend Thulani. Every time he tried to run, he felt his feet sinking deeper into the sand, stopping him dead.

As the days progressed, it became increasingly clear to his parents that something was bothering Sizwe; but he refused to open up. They pampered him with presents – a new bicycle, a pair of roller skates, a new hi-fi system. But none of these things could slake the thirst that seemed to have taken possession of him. He hardly ever ate, spent most of the time in his room buried in notebooks. Now and then they would stumble upon him sitting at his writing table, staring into space, with a pen poised impatiently over a blank piece of paper.

His teachers, who had known him as a conscientious pupil, started sending letters of complaint to his parents about his lack of concentration, his sloppy schoolwork, and rude demeanour.

The mid-year exams caught him by surprise. But still he didn't panic, did not study overtime. Which is why everyone, including himself, was surprised when he came top of the entire matriculation class at his school.

Buoyed by this success, he spent the June holidays reworking some of the short stories he had written a few years ago. He immediately sent out the pieces to both literary journals and consumer magazines. Two of the four pieces were snapped up by mass-circulation magazines. The two literary journals he had approached both rejected his work. He paused only briefly to wallow in self-pity, but soon moved ahead and continued writing.

By the time the schools re-opened, he had become a celebrity not only at his school but in the entire neighbourhood, which had seen his name in the popular magazines.

He was back in form, scoring high marks in all his tests, and jovial in class; the transformation reached a peak when he received a letter of acceptance from the University of Natal. The institution undertook to reserve him a place pending his final results at the end of the year. This was enough to put more fire in his belly to work hard.

Before the year was over, the school governing body had made some funds available to Sizwe and a handful of other pupils with literary inclinations, to start a student magazine. The first issue carried a couple of his own short pieces, and one long one by Vusi Mntungwa. Members of the editorial board objected to the inclusion of a piece by an established writer who had been published numerous times in serious, grown-up journals. As editor, Sizwe overruled them.

'We are very proud of you, boy,' his mother told him as the family sat at the dinner table one night.

'Thank you, mom.'

'Heek-heek-heek,' his father laughed, 'I think those boys who beat him up the other night taught him a good lesson to keep off the streets, and concentrate on his books.'

Twenty-Three
The Mayor's Bowl

All the prominent citizens, movers and shakers of Exclusive Park were gathered at the local community hall that night. The occasion was to celebrate the excellent matric results that had been achieved by Sizwe's school, Exclusive High. Needless to say, he had come out tops and was the toast of the evening.

Dressed in a new cream suit bought specially for this glittering event, Sizwe was flanked by his parents. Not that he objected much to their presence, but his eyes were roving all over the throng of humanity flowing into the hall. The hall had been elaborately decorated for the occasion. There were ribbons, flowers and balloons all over the place. He was impatiently trying to locate his sweetheart Nolitha, whom he had invited.

Tables covered with gleaming white tablecloths were neatly arranged around the floor. Two long tables had been set on the stage. This was where the mayor, his wife, some dignitaries, and the top matriculant of the year – in other words, Sizwe – were to sit and dine, while hoi polloi dined at the lesser tables below. The night had been billed as the Mayor's Dinner in Honour of Educational Excellence. But if truth be told, the mayor was a mere figurehead. The person who had arranged, organised and financed the whole night was none other than Lettie Motaung, the owner of Paradise Road. She was ordinarily a generous person, but her extreme generosity this time had been influenced by the fact that her son Kokoroshe had done extremely well. She was proud.

'Good evening, my neighbours!' the mayor greeted the boys who served as ushers as he walked grandly towards the stage with his wife.

The mayor was a gregarious man who was short of stature, so round he sometimes looked like one of those huge wheels of cheese. His rotundity could be blamed on his love of food and beverages. For a man his size, his voice was extremely squeaky. It became even squeakier as the effects of alcohol took possession of him.

As soon as the mayor arrived at his table and sat down, he began sampling some snacks set out in front of him: wedges of cheese, crackers, slices of ham.

By the time Sizwe was ordered to go and get seated beside the mayor, he still hadn't located his sweetheart. His parents had been kindly asked to sit at a table not too far from the mayoral table.

'So, my little neighbour,' the mayor greeted Sizwe brightly, shaking his hand, 'let me shake the hand that shook the country. Hahahaha!' The mayor laughed with his head back, his false teeth almost falling out. Before coming here, Sizwe had been warned about the good mayor's teeth which had a mind of their own, but he had dismissed those comments as mere jokes.

'Yes, good evening, sir' Sizwe beamed back, 'it's good to make your acquaintance at last. You once promised to come and watch our soccer side playing against Highlanders from Johannesburg, but we never were lucky enough to have you grace our little soccer competition, sir. But I suppose as mayor you've got so many fishes to fry.'

Any other man would have been embarrassed. Not the mayor. He merely threw his head back. 'You're right there, my neighbour. Mayors have so many fishes to fry. Big fishes. Hahahaha! Now, by the way, my little neighbour, what are you going to study next year, what do you want to be?'

'Journalist.'

'Ah, newsman! Black newsmen played a pivotal role in the liberation of this country by exposing the horrors and the brutality of apartheid. Mind you, we are not entirely free yet, but with the release of Nelson Mandela last year we can see hope on the horizon. Those of us who move in the top corridors of power know that possibly next year or at least in 1994 we will have a black government in control. All thanks to the selfless work of black journalists. But now, son, don't you think there are other better things to study? With the demise of apartheid, surely more doors will be open for us black people – in the fields of chemistry, aviation, banking. You know, fields that are the cornerstones of a civilised economy. Not to say journalism doesn't matter, but it's a dead end for a bright boy like you. I believe you did well at maths, business economics, accounting... I mean, get real, my neighbour, hahahaha!'

Sizwe was no longer listening because he had just spotted Nolitha walking his way, hand in hand with Kokoroshe. She was stunning in a silver-grey evening dress that he had bought her a week ago specially for this evening. He watched them being ushered to a table not too far from his parents. His father spotted Nolitha and waved. She waved back. Now Kokoroshe looked this way; they waved at each other.

The principal of Exclusive High congratulated her top students, wished them well with their tertiary education. As a parting shot, she said: 'It's a pity teaching methods at our black schools are still in the doldrums. Of all the pupils gathered here, with their glowing results, we are missing one boy with brains. He was betrayed by our educational system. No matter where he is now, Thulani Tembe, who is probably known to all of you, will be sorely missed. From the bottom of my heart, I can say with all humility that that boy, whatever happens to him in future, can rightfully blame us. He didn't leave school simply because he was a bad apple. We let him down. But wherever he is, I wish him luck.'

More speeches followed, but members did not pay much attention to these as they were still digesting the principal's last words.

The mayor got up to deliver his keynote address. It was a speech whose main thrust was to encourage the young people to take centre stage in the affairs of running the country politically, economically, and so on. 'The white man is on his way out, are we ready to take over? Taking over means changing the education so it doesn't go on betraying young people, as the principal illustrated early. Taking over means creating sustainable jobs for our people. Taking over means building houses for our people. Taking over means looking after our elderly. Taking over doesn't mean moving into the white man's house and sleeping with the missus.'

Now he threw his head back and laughed out loud, with the audience joining him. He continued laughing until his false teeth jumped out of his mouth. He tried to catch them in mid-air, but missed. They plunged into a punch bowl nearby. He stole a glance at his wife, who was looking ahead sternly. He dipped his hand into the punch bowl, fishing about for the wayward dentures. He licked them briefly before putting them back where they belonged, all of this to more uproarious laughter. But he did this so quickly, that people soon forgot what had happened and listened hard to his well-thought-out speech.

As the mayor continued, Sizwe's mind flew back to the past when he had listened to one of his father's lectures: 'My boy, unlike most of us, you are lucky to have reached your level of education. You might not realise it now, but education is the spear, the weapon that you will use to pierce your way through throngs of the black man's enemies: ignorance, poverty, joblessness, insecurity. With education, you will defeat these enemies that have made our lives as miserable as they are right now. Achievement in high school education is only the beginning. You have to go further, not only for the material benefits that will accrue from the education; knowledge and wisdom are by themselves a reward. I am not an educated man myself, but when I sit with some of the educated people I begin to value the education I was deprived of. Pick this spear up, and forge ahead.'

After eating their three-course meal, people got down to drinking. The mayor was now walking about the hall, mingling with his neighbours, as he preferred to call the people. It was noteworthy that people were giving the mayor's punch bowl a wide berth. One well-dressed gentleman who had been sitting at the cheap tables walked drunkenly to the stage, his eyes trained on the punch bowl. He picked up a glass and was in the process of pouring himself a helping when one of the dignitaries admonished him: 'No, leave that bowl alone. It belongs to the mayor.'

'But the mayor is also a human being! I am also a human being. Didn't we all fight for this democracy, for this equality?'

The dignitaries sniggered behind the well-dressed man's back as he gorged himself on the punch. Floating visibly on the surface of the drink were crumbs and other residue from the mayor's teeth. The people shall share, the Freedom Charter taught us.

Twenty-Four

Talking White, Talking Black, Talking Trash

Sizwe had not, except perhaps on TV, seen so many white people gathered at the same place at the same time. There were all kinds of them: those with dark black hair and matching dark eyes, whom he assumed were Greeks or Portuguese. There were those with white hair – or blond hair, as he had been corrected by those who knew these things. They had green eyes, blue eyes. There were those with flaming red hair. Brown hair. Hair spangled with so many colours they looked like peacocks.

The confidence and self-assuredness he had cultivated over the years, always ahead of his peers when it came to things to do with education or the written word, suddenly went out of the window. All at once he was a scared black boy in the face of the white world. He stood in front of the registration offices and watched the sea of white humanity raging.

He had been told that in the past the university only admitted white students, but that over the years it had become mixed. Now he had been standing there for more than ten minutes but had yet to see a black face. Maybe he had been given the wrong information, he decided. Maybe the university was still white. He didn't want to get into trouble. He had heard of horrible things that had befallen black people who had had the temerity to put their black feet on holy ground reserved for white people.

Standing there, looking at these unapproachable white faces who didn't even seem to notice him, to think he might be in need of help, made him feel a tightening in the stomach. He suddenly felt dizzy. He looked up at the sky. There were doves flitting merrily, as if laughing at him. The sky was blue, cloudless.

'Yo, brother, whassup?' He was roused from his reverie by what sounded like a black voice, a black voice modelled on the hip-hop shit that he'd seen on TV. 'Yo, man, you tripping, huh!'

He looked around and saw his salvation. She was clearly black, in fact darker than he was. She wore her hair in dreadlocks, earrings in all the impossible places: nose, lower lip, even in her belly button, which was exposed proudly. In addition to the skimpy white top she had on, she had the rest of her covered in a long denim skirt that reached her ankles. She had on a pair of sandals. She carried a small leather handbag. He smiled at her. But now he realised that her face was not as jovial as the voice had sounded.

'Patrick, let's go,' the woman said, which came out as: Pootrick less goo!

'Yo, bro, I'm talkin' to you, huh,' the voice came again.

Then Sizwe noticed that standing next to the black girl was a tall white young man in baggy jeans threatening to fall off his tiny body, sneakers and a Lakers shirt. He also had on a Lakers cap worn backwards.

'You seem lost, bro,' the young white man spoke again, and now Sizwe realised that the pseudo-black American accent was for his benefit. 'You goin' someplace fast, or you still admiring the scenery?'

'Oh, uhm,' Sizwe cleared his throat, approaching the two apparitions. 'I am looking for the administration building. I am a first-year student.'

'No worry, my brother,' said the young white man, 'I'll take you directly to the registration office.'

'But, Patrick, we have no time. Let's go!' Boot Pootrick we hoove no time. Less goo.

'Man, Patrick McGuinness is the name,' the young man said by way of introduction. 'This here is my queen Thembi. And what's your moniker, dude?'

The two men shook hands. Sizwe extended his hand towards

the queen, but she simply said, 'Hello.' And looked away, her arms folded across her tiny breasts.

'I'm leaving you now, Patrick. Getting late for my meeting.' She stormed away.

'See you later, doll,' Patrick called after her. Then he turned to him, 'Come, I'll take you directly to the office. This place is a maze. Very intimidating for first years.' The street twang had disappeared. He was sounding like a white South African again. Sizwe was glad because he could understand him now.

'You see, I don't understand darkies sometimes,' Patrick was saying. 'Instead of getting together and pulling together, they have become so individualistic they make us whities look like egalitarian communists who share ideas, help each other up the ladder. Take Thembi's performance a few minutes ago, for example. I've seen it so many times before. Darkies who are seasoned denizens on predominantly white campuses are always dismissive, even hostile, towards black newcomers, as if they feel that what is rightfully theirs, what their parents strived to achieve for them, is being given to undeserving darkies who are riding on the ticket of freedom, affirmative action. Man, I don't know if I am making sense.'

He took out a packet of cigarettes, offered Sizwe one. Sizwe was not an habitual smoker at the time, but he thought that turning down the offer would seem rude. They smoked.

'You see, Thembi's a good bitch, but...'

'Why are you calling her a bitch?'

That jolted Patrick. Then he smiled, 'Yo, nigger, where you from, huh?' He continued smiling, pointing an accusing finger at Sizwe. 'Nah, nah, nigger you from the sticks; you don't dig the lingo.'

'Man, don't call me a nigger,' he raised his voice, attracting the attention of the other white people in the queue.

Patrick sighed, and started speaking South African English again: 'As I was saying, Thembi is actually a good girl. It's just that she feels under pressure to fit within this environment. So she has changed her English diction so she sounds like some white girl from Sandton. She's been my girlfriend for two years now, but I get the feeling she hasn't come to terms with the fact that there are black people out there whose parents are well-to-do enough to send their kids to a predominantly white university. With more black people coming in here, she seems to be losing her status as "the only darkie", or "one of the few darkies", the flavour-of-the-month status, if you get my drift.'

'Why are you telling me all of this?'

'Yo, bro, are you always this intense? Man, I am trying to be friendly, trying to give you the low-down on what's going on in this place. You giving me aggravation instead of appreciation. Man, tha's not cool.'

'Thanks for your consideration, but maybe I should find these things out myself.'

'That's a dangerous approach. You see, me, the darkies don't like me because I get on well with the black dolls. The honkies don't like me either 'cos they say I'm letting them down, trying to be black, always voting with the black students at SRC meetings. Me, I go to hip-hop when my white brothers are getting high and puking and smashing each other with baseball bats at their rowdy rock sessions.'

They stood in the queue getting to know each other, talking about this and that. Sizwe's turn finally came. For his part, he had not decided what he would be studying. In the forms he filled in, he entered one commercial subject – accounting – because it was easy, and English 1, philosophy, communication science, because they fascinated him. He went through the rigmarole of registration and was assigned a room at one of the new hostels.

Patrick gave him directions to his new home. Patrick told him about a campus pub where they could meet later, 'so we can shoot the breeze, chew the fat, man, know what I'm saying,' said Patrick as he sauntered away, pimp-roll style as Sizwe had seen dirty thugs do in the townships. The dude would take a regular step with one leg, then drag the other on the second step so that, to the uninitiated eye, he looked like some kind of cripple, or a person with legs which were unequal in length. It was called Ukubhampa – the Bounce, or the Pimp Roll, as the Americans called it.

Interesting, thought Sizwe, a white boy trying to be black, with a black girlfriend at pains to sound white. University was going to be interesting indeed. This much he said in the first letters he wrote to his parents and to Kokoroshe, who had been trooped off to the University of Cape Town where he was doing a commerce degree: 'Take it or leave it, and don't give me that shit about speech and drama,' his mother Sis Lettie Motaung had said with finality.

Twenty-Five
Higher Learning

Sizwe

This girl Thembi looked alluring in her tight jeans and figure-hugging top today. The yellow turban she had on was a head-turner. I've never seen anyone wearing such a combination and getting away with it. Not in a long time have I felt so attracted to a girl. But she got on my nerves in our philosophy class. She laughed out loud every time one of the black students mispronounced an English word.

I bumped into her at the pub. I said hi. She looked through me, and continued laughing with her white friends. But even that pout of hers touched my heart, turned me on. How do I even begin to unburden my heart to her when she is refusing to even acknowledge my presence? There surely must be a way of getting to her.

As for Patrick, I think he is too much of a dreamer. I've never seen him in any class. I know he is a senior, but he seems to hang around more at the pub or inside the offices of the SRC. He has asked me to join the editorial team of the student publication. Maybe I should give it a try. But I must work hard at my studies.

Thembi

My parents were thrilled to hear that I was going out with Patrick McGuinness. A gallant Irishman, my father called him. Then he started regaling me and Mama with stories about an Irish town called Limerick. A town of poets and writers, he said. Irish people were like black people. They had suffered just like us black people.

But they are still white, my mother countered later on, to me.

They are better than these black monkeys in our country, monkeys who don't want to work and blame all their misfortune on the white government, she said. Look where we are right now, despite our black colour. We took it upon ourselves to work hard, that's why I have no truck with these monkey faces who are forever whingeing about oppression, apartheid. Damn! It makes you wish you were born another colour, in another country! I can't wait to see Patrick McGuinness sitting with us at dinner table.

You say he is doing his master's in Irish literature, he must be a bright boy, my father had said.

But it's never too late to steer him in the right direction, my mother jumped in. Get him to do some commercial subjects, she said. What's the use of having a husband with all the theories about literature and the world, but with no commercial sense, and therefore no means of taking good care of you financially? You tell me that!

This was a year ago when I mentioned his name. But up to now my parents still haven't met him. Now they are getting impatient to see 'our future son-in-law', as mother calls him.

But I am scared I am going to disappoint them. Patrick, though white he is, is not the type of son-in-law a mother would appreciate. He goes too hard on this black thing of his, number one. Number two, he doesn't dress like any educated man I've ever seen. I don't think my parents would approve of his dress sense. He doesn't own a decent pair of shoes, for example, let alone a jacket. Number three, he is getting deeper and deeper into booze. Every time I see him he reeks of booze. I don't think he goes to classes any more. He is spending way too much time at the SRC offices or working twenty-four hours at the offices of the student magazine. What is he going to gain out of that, I wonder. Expending your energies and intellect on a stupid student magazine! But still, my parents want to meet him. Urgently now. Something has to be done.

Patrick

My money is running low. Which is bad news. I am being drawn back inexorably to my past. The streets. Back to the streets where the money is. Back to the streets where the excitement is. Back to the streets where the blood is. The streets are getting more dangerous now, but what choice do I have? Something's gotta give, know what I'm saying? Thinking about excitement, I remember one of my first experiences on the street. It was one balmy evening, around 7 p.m., give or take. For a Friday, the streets in Braamfontein were relatively deserted. I had been walking down Biccard, then moving to De Korte, where I normally met the tricks. They were mostly middle-aged to old men. Men with fat tummies, big jowls. Men who, no matter how often they washed, had a nauseating smell about them. Some of them were regulars at the nearby German restaurant. Sated with sauerkraut, eisbein and some other shitty German food, they would prowl the street in search of one of us. Sometimes if they couldn't get a boy, they would resort to girls. But boys were their first preference. I was the first white boy to walk the streets in these parts.

Initially, the tricks were suspicious, thinking I was a cop working undercover. But soon I was in demand. I was white, therefore hygienically clean and trustworthy. The tricks could rest assured that I would not turn on them and rob them of their money, stab them or some shit like that.

Anyway, my first trick was this extremely thin guy with big spectacles almost framing his entire face, each lens like a TV screen – hahahaha! – a big Greek nose, and a surprisingly deep voice for one so thin. I had given up walking and was now sitting on one of the benches, tired, hungry, angry at myself for being such a miserable sod.

He walked up the street for the first time, throwing furtive glances at me. When he reached the traffic lights, he turned back and walked this way again. Even from where I was sitting I could see his erection behind his loose trousers. But he still couldn't muster the courage to ask if I had what he was looking for. I was wearing tight-fitting jeans, a fashionable gaudy disco dancing jacket – one of those flimsy affairs that look expensive under the stroboscopic lights of a nightclub. My hair was still thick then, combed carefully back, and gelled so it stuck to my skull.

'I've got what you looking for, mister,' I said nonchalantly as he approached me again.

'What do you take me for? A drug addict?'

'It's not drugs you looking for, I know that.'

'Fuck off, or I'll call the police.'

'No need to be aggro, my man. I can make you very happy – all night if you want.'

He paused, looked at me, looked up and down the street, and said, 'Okay, let's go.'

We walked a block, and finally arrived at a block of flats. His flat was on the ground floor. He unlocked the door. We walked into the clean flat with an array of African art.

'You like it?' he asked when he realised I was staring at a West African mask dominating what seemed like his lounge.

'Exquisite.' Then I started talking knowledgeably about art.

'Are you a student then?'

'Yes.'

After that there were no further questions. I was glad. Many of these tricks sometimes could act weird. With their erections throbbing, they would launch into long speeches about why such a good-looking, clean, educated boy shouldn't be walking the streets. Then they would still go ahead and fuck you. After all the sanctimonious preaching. I mean! Come on! Get a life, dickhead!

This dickhead here didn't waste his or my time. He got down to it as soon as he had closed the door to his flat. He stroked my face, took me to the bathroom where we massaged each other in the hot bath. Later we retired to the bedroom where we did it.

Later, he was so exhausted he fell asleep. I got up quietly, got dressed, went through his pockets, took his watch, carefully removed the West African mask from its perch on the wall.

I was already in the street when I heard him bawl from the

entrance of the flat: 'Thief! Thief! Stop thief!'

A group of about six white men who were walking down the pavement, two of them legless with alcohol, wondered aloud: 'What the hell is he talking about? What thief?'

You see, think thief, think black. Not a good-looking white boy on his way home from a nightclub, or art gallery.

Anyway, there were many other experiences after that. I made a lot of money. Then Thembi came into my life. I continued walking the streets to make enough money to entertain her. The demanding materialistic bitch. She insisted on wearing a new outfit for every party we went to. On two occasions we went to funerals of her relatives. Even then she insisted on new outfits for each of the funerals. She is so selfish and full of herself, you'd think her pussy was made of gold.

As time went by, there were turf wars between numerous pimps. The one who ultimately won the turf war was a guy called Daddy Cool, a mean bastard. His boys had asked me to join them, or leave the neighbourhood. I decided to quit the job. I had enough money anyway.

But now my money is gone. I've been thinking about joining Daddy Cool's crew. But my heart of hearts has told me: Patrick, go back to the streets and do your own shit. Fuck Daddy Cool. It's me being fucked. Not his ass.

Twenty-Six
Men of Letters

'Doll,' Patrick was saying, taking a long drag from his zol, 'this is good shit. This Vusi Mntungwa fellow can write. You say he is a friend of yours? Where is he now?'

'Ag,' Sizwe said, 'it's a long story. He's somewhere out there in the world. He left me all his writings. Said I could do with them as I please.'

The zol passed from hand to hand as Sizwe told the story of his growing up with Thulani Tembe, how they had competed as writers and thinkers. He hadn't meant to be so honest, but he had said it: he had competed against his friend Thulani Tembe and had felt defeated.

They were in Patrick's room. It was surprisingly neat for a smoker, a drinker and one who walked around with the words 'Streetwise devil-may-care' emblazoned on his forehead. There was a tiny bed, a wardrobe, a writing desk in one corner, on top of which was an ancient typewriter. And there were two bookshelves with a variety of books from fiction to heavy tomes on literary theory and history. Then there was a cupboard bursting with unfinished manuscripts. Finally there was a small bar fridge stocked with beer. Right now, they had each demolished six cans of beer and were still going strong. They were sitting on cushions scattered on the carpeted floor. Sticks of incense were burning in what looked like some kind of shrine dominated by a statuette of Buddha. In the middle of the room was a huge takeaway seafood platter – prawns, linefish, calamari and fresh oysters – which they were slowly, systematically stuffing into their mouths.

'For some reason I don't think this fellow Vusi Mntungwa exists.

I think you wrote these stories yourself. You are using the name Vusi Mntungwa as a shield to protect your ego from criticism. Your thinking is like this: If the literary critics out there tear this Vusi Mntungwa to shreds, it's fine because he is not me. But deep in your heart of hearts, you know you wrote the shit. I agree that the stuff that you've written under your own name is different from the stuff ostensibly written by Vusi Mntungwa. In fact the two are not comparable. I think you are trying to explore two different voices, to see which works best, which gets more appeal. But the novel manuscript that you showed me, although written by Vusi Mntungwa, has echoes of Sizwe Dube. I don't know if I am making sense.'

Patrick was fairly close to the truth. Sizwe had taken an unfinished novel manuscript from Thulani's collection and worked painstakingly hard to bring the unfinished story to an end. He had tried hard to make his writing style close to that of his friend Thulani's. But right now, he was not going to tell Patrick all of this.

'You know, Patrick, you are getting on my nerves. I don't know what I should do to get you to believe that Vusi Mntungwa is a pseudonymn of a person who exists, who's out there in the big world.'

'I'm afraid you'll have to prove it to me.'

'Patrick, why are you playing all this hip-hop shit, all these darkies barking instead of singing? Can't you play something with people actually singing? If that's too hard for you, play some instrumental jazz, something smooth and civilised. Not all this nigga-this, nigga-that shit. This is just not music, I don't care who says what.'

'The brothers are sending the message to The Man, motherfucker! Telling Hymie where to get off, ya dig!'

'Our Jamaican brothers can send the same message to The Man, as you call him, more elegantly, more musically,' Sizwe said, inserting into the system a Culture CD.

'Reggae is out, man. Hip-hop is da thing, know what I'm saying?'

It was now time for Patrick to tell his life story. Sizwe listened carefully, sipping his beer and rolling another joint. He had started growing his hair into dreadlocks.

He was startled when Patrick got to that part about walking the streets as a male prostitute. 'But why did you do that?'

'Man, I needed money. When my parents died, they left me nothing. After they'd died I moved from one set of relatives to the next until I finished high school. Then I got a scholarship for my first year at university. When I decided to change from commerce to the arts, my benefactor, a petroleum company, withdrew their benevolence. I then had to raise my own money.'

'Tell me you have stopped.'

'I have, yes, I have. Sorry to upset you, man.' Now tears were rushing down his cheeks.

This was an awkward moment for Sizwe. He didn't know what to do. In the movies he would have moved closer to his friend, gave him a comforting hug. But this was not in the movies. This was real life.

'I'm sorry to hear that, man,' he said quietly.

He found himself thinking about his friend Thulani, and how they sometimes walked down the street hand in hand, sometimes hugging when either of them was sad, going through a hard time. Those had been impulsive moments, unrehearsed expressions of brotherly love, friendship.

Now, he found himself moving close to his friend, to embrace him. They stayed in a tight embrace for sometime, Joseph Hall, the lead singer of Culture, singing in the background: 'Zion is a holy place... sin shall not enter there.'

To Patrick, contact triggered a sexual response; it evoked cinematic flashes of other bodies he'd embraced, eyes he'd looked into, lips he'd marvelled at. When he caressed Sizwe's face, the latter didn't recoil. Soon they were kissing, and later moved into bed.

Much later, Sizwe lay on his back staring at the ceiling. He was waiting for the feeling of strangeness, of disgust, to engulf him.

A century later, the feeling hadn't even quivered on the horizon. What did come to his mind was the time he and Thulani had had sex with Nolitha in the bush. Done with her, the two boys had walked home hand in hand. From his perspective, Sizwe had never felt closer to Thulani than that day. In fact he had felt so close to his friend it felt he was him. He squeezed his hand until Thulani faked a vicious cough, which gave him an excuse to release his hand from Sizwe's firm grasp.

'When I was young, if I made soup...'

The encounters between Sizwe and Patrick became more frequent in the weeks that followed.

Within months, then, the rumour that the two were confirmed lovers gained currency on campus. The news was possibly fuelled by Patrick himself as a way of politely ending the relationship with Thembi. She was becoming a pest, demanding him to come and meet her parents. The stories Thembi told him about his parents conjured in his mind a couple he wouldn't be seen dead talking to, let alone having them as his parents-in-law. Ag, puleezz, doll!

To his surprise, Sizwe did not feel ashamed of these developments; in fact, he derived a morbid satisfaction from Thembi's suffering, which was there for everyone to see.

She had started talking Zulu to other darkies, but the darkies didn't know what to do with her, so they fed her booze and dagga so that she always ended up in a drunken stupor at all social gatherings, vomiting, and waking up in a stranger's bed the next morning.

Twenty-Seven
The Oneness of Two In Three

The story on the front page of *The Star* caught Sizwe's attention; it told briefly and unemotionally about how one Patrick McGuinness, a student at Wits University and a prominent up-and-coming writer, had been attacked. He had been stabbed and bludgeoned with blunt objects, and was left for dead in Braamfontein.

Quickly, Sizwe phoned the police to find out which hospital Patrick had been taken to. He was summoned to the police station, where he explained his relationship with the injured patient. Only then was he allowed into the ward where his friend was recuperating.

Sizwe was disgusted that Patrick had continued walking the streets behind his back, hence the attack on him by what he thought was a group of rival male prostitutes. But Sizwe was there for him during his recuperation at Johannesburg General Hospital. He brought him fruit and reading material. He sat at his bedside telling him stories, lifting his spirits.

When Patrick was finally discharged, they moved in together in a house in Brixton. The garden was sheer bliss – a rockery with bougainvillea, white dahlias, carnations, violets; a profusion of colour that attracted colourful birds and bees in summer. The lawn was evergreen. At the back of the house was a tiny orchard bursting with peaches, mulberries, and lemons. Bees buzzed and birds chirped about the branches, picking at the fruit.

It was in the orchard that Sizwe and Patrick would sit and talk story ideas, smoking and drinking beer. Sometimes they would have friends over for a braai, both gay and straight people.

They found themselves making love under the peach trees

one moonlit night. The aroma of ripening fruit was alluring. The noise of night creatures added a romantic feel to the atmosphere. Mosquitoes and moths dive-bombed their faces, but they persisted. Sated, covered in sweat, they collapsed on the towel spread on the grass and stared at the patches of light between the canopy of tree branches. They didn't say a word to each other, just stared into nothingness, breathing quietly, enjoying each other's company.

Then Patrick said, 'You know, I have an idea. How about you writing an essay for one of the literary journals, an essay entitled "The Politics of Being Gay in the Black South African Community"? I mean, that will get people talking, how this young, straight black dude suddenly finds the urge to come out unashamedly in the face of a barrage of vilifications and insults.'

'Lovely idea. Maybe we can get the editors to publish it alongside your "Confessions of a White Male Prostitute in a Changing South Africa"?'

'Come on, man, I didn't mean it that way.'

'Sounded patronising to me.'

They helped each other up from the ground and walked back into the house.

Back home in Durban, no one was aware of the changes that had taken place in Sizwe's life. They were just proud that his name seemed to be all over the place in newspapers as he had become an important social commentator. He continued to publish his short stories steadily in the literary journals. They showered him with praises in the letters they wrote to him – especially Nolitha, who was the most prolific of writers, even surpassing Sizwe's own mother.

With Kokoroshe gone to university, his mother had felt so lonely she'd asked Nolitha to come and live with her. By this time, Lovey had become even more unreliable. She would disappear from home for weeks on end, no matter how many dire threats she received from her mother. Not only had Kokoroshe's mother taken Nolitha under her wing, she put her back to school. She was now in Standard Nine, she announced happily in one of the letters she wrote to Sizwe.

This news filled Sizwe with joy. He had long been planning to help finance Nolitha's studies, but the recent turbulence in his life had impacted negatively on many of his plans. Yet Sizwe was now torn between Nolitha and Patrick.

No sooner had Patrick recovered from his injuries than he landed a job with one of the book publishers in Johannesburg. He joined the publishing house as one of a troop of readers.

With Patrick at work the whole day, Sizwe resumed his studies with renewed vigour. Back on track, he started writing for the magazines again. There were book reviews, opinion pieces, and the odd short story. Sometimes he got out-of-town assignments which gave him the opportunity to see the many different parts of the country he had long been planning to visit. However, the downside to these trips was that he was always alone, unable to share the poetic beauty of the land with the person who mattered most in his life.

It was while he was on one of these out-of-town jaunts that he received a call in his hotel room late one night. He was in Cape Town, covering an airshow for one of the national aviation magazines. The caller was Patrick.

'Doll, I can't sleep. It's way past midnight, but I am tossing and turning here. My heart is heavy with guilt.'

'Why? What happened?'

'I know you're not going to like this but…'

'Don't fuckin' tell me you were on the street again. Don't tell me that!' He was fully awake now, standing naked and barefoot on the thick carpet, his dick hardening beyond control. It always did that when he was angry. 'Don't tell me you've been fucking around again, because I'm gonna kill you. Murder you. Grind you to a pulp.'

'But, doll, you're not listening…'

'Don't fucking doll me! What do I have to listen to? What have you done? I know you, you are beginning to turn into a fucking druggie and I don't like that one bit. Not one fucking bit! You think I don't realise that you're not only smoking weed, but have now graduated to snorting cocaine. Snort-snort-snort. Like a pig. Like a fucking pig and you think I haven't noticed it?'

There was a long silence on the other end. He could hear himself breathing hard, really worked up, his hand clasped tightly around the neck of the telephone receiver, strangling the poor piece of plastic.

'Can I speak now?'

'Yes.'

'At the office today... okay, let me take a deep breath, let me rephrase that. Today I had a meeting with Sheree, the senior editor. I showed her a couple of the short stories you've written and asked her if she would like to publish them as a collection. To tell you the truth, I gave the collection to her eleven weeks ago already, but only today did she come back to me. She loved the stories, and expressed a mild interest in publishing them. A collection of short stories, even the most brilliant ones, doesn't make much commercial sense. Especially if the author is a household name. To get to the point, then, Sheree said she would like to have a meeting with you, with us. She can't wait to discuss the novel manuscript. It really knocked her socks off, the novel manuscript did...'

'What novel manuscript are you talking about?'

'"The Oneness of Two in Three" – you know, the Vusi Mntungwa manuscript.'

'You fucking moffie bitch! You limp dick! What did I say to you about that manuscript? Didn't I tell you it's off bounds, it's not to be shown to anyone?'

'I'm sorry, man, I thought I was helping. This thing is a kicker. It'll open doors for your future projects. That's what I told you the other time, remember. "Oneness" is your foot in the door, sweetheart. She wants to publish it like yesterday. And she's talking big bucks, doll.'

'I'm not interested if she's going to offer a billion rand for it. That fucking manuscript is sacred, not to be touched by anyone, not a publisher, not God himself. The first time I saw you I realised you were a fake, a patronising piece of shit trying to talk black! A fucking manipulator. You whites are all the same. Every time we give you a hand of friendship, you chop it off. Fucking patronising pieces of shit.'

'Doll, is it a colour thing now? I thought we were reading these things from the same page. Is it a colour thing now?' Click! The phone died.

Sizwe stood rooted to the ground, temples pounding. He needed fresh air. He put on his jeans, socks, sneakers and T-shirt, and left his room.

The streets were quiet, with an occasional car driving past. The surf was pounding across the road from the hotel. He started walking without knowing where he was going, the cool vapour from the sea sticking to his face.

For the past few months he had been working so hard that he had almost forgotten the existence of the Vusi Mntungwa manuscript. In fact, even the face of his friend Thulani had become a vague, distant memory. But all of a sudden Thulani had once again become larger than life in his mind's eye. He would have preferred that things could return to the period of the past months when he had been revelling in his journalistic prowess, basking in the glory bestowed upon him by people who thought he was one of the most promising writers around. He had been feeling very good about himself, until this!

The mere mention of the Vusi Mntungwa manuscripts had sucked from his body and soul every ounce of confidence and pride he had. He thought he had rid his system of his abominable friend Thulani, but this spectre from his past kept haunting him, dictating to him what he had to think about, how he had to live his life, what his priorities should be.

'When I was young, if I made soup...'

Early the following day, he flew back to Johannesburg. He took a cab from Johannesburg International, arriving at their house just as Patrick was leaving for work. Sizwe had calmed down overnight. They kissed and exchanged pleasantries over coffee.

'Listen,' he said to Patrick, 'you can carry on to the office. I'll join you guys for lunch so we can talk this shit over.'

Much relieved, Patrick smiled: 'Ah, I see you've come to your senses now, doll!'

Twenty-Eight
A Cracker of a Story

Sizwe always started reading his newspaper of choice, the *Cape Mail*, from the features section. No one could blame him for this habit because, as a regular contributor there, he derived pleasure in seeing his name in print, seeing his ideas, words, phrases, in black and white, and wondering how many other people elsewhere in the country were doing the same, getting immersed in the lyrical beauty of his writing, eating from his hand, so to speak.

Done with the features section, he would jump to the opinion pages, which always got his thinking machine chugging, getting ready for the day. Having ranted and raved against the opinions he read, he would then shuttle back to the front page for the news of the day, and then flip the paper over to have a cursory glance at the sports pages.

But this morning was different. It was different because the front page was dominated by the face of his friend Thulani Tembe, under the headline 'Face of a Monster!' The caption identified the man as Freedom Cele. He looked long and hard at the picture and was convinced it was the face of his friend. He had not seen him in more than ten years, true, but it was him all right – proud forehead, the nose that reminded him of Thulani's father, the reverend. The man in the picture had a pencil moustache, and laugh lines that ran along the sides of his nose. This is how the fun-loving, always-laughing Thulani would look after all the years he hadn't seen him. The jowls were those of a well-fed man. He had been eating a lot over the past few years in his solitary journey into the unknown, Sizwe thought. His shoulders were those of a regular visitor to the gym, round, well-built.

It was the man's eyes that disturbed Sizwe most. They were indeed the bright eyes of Thulani, yes, but now they had that distant, forlorn look in them, as if the man was staring somewhere into the future, into some darkness that only he could see.

The story told in gory detail how the man in the picture, Freedom Cele, of Khayelitsha, Cape Town, had been found guilty of 153 charges of rape, kidnapping and indecent assault. He had been sentenced to a total of 300 years in jail. And so on.

He stopped reading and went to a pile of other daily newspapers that Patrick had left on top of the washing machine. All three Johannesburg dailies led with the same story about the eviction of people squatting illegally on private land near the airport. But each also carried on their front pages a bottom-of-the-page story about Freedom Cele – all without a picture. He looked over and over at the picture and was left convinced that this was his friend Thulani.

He rushed to the bedroom, where they had their telephone. He dialled the offices of the newspaper and asked to speak to the court reporter whose byline appeared above the story. The reporter confirmed that the man in the picture was indeed Freedom Cele. The story had been running for the past month, of course. But it was only on the day of sentencing that the presiding judge granted newspapers permission to publish the picture.

'Of course, of course,' Sizwe said, and thanked the reporter. He put the phone back on its cradle. He sat on the bed and thought very hard. Then it dawned on him that his friend had changed his name.

He reached for the telephone directory and looked for the number of the prison where the newspaper said Freedom Cele would serve his time. He phoned the prison. The person on the other end was courteous, giving him the postal address and warning him that some of the mail was opened and could be censored before being handed over to inmates.

He thanked her and said goodbye. He walked slowly towards the kitchen, put the kettle on. The water boiled and he made himself a cup of coffee, all the time thinking carefully.

He thought of taking the next flight to Cape Town to see his friend, commiserate with him, but quickly decided against it. It hadn't been Thulani's idea to be found by those who knew him, which is why he had changed his name. He decided to give his friend the breathing space he needed. An idea was taking shape in his head.

Next, he phoned Thulani's mother at her place of work. She was happy to hear his voice. They talked at length about nothing in particular. Her tone of voice didn't betray alarm or sadness. Then he phoned his own parents. They were both happy to hear from him. Again, they didn't seem to have seen the picture of his friend under the name of Freedom Cele. He said goodbye, put the phone down, and mulled over this.

It suddenly dawned on him that only the Cape papers would have carried the picture of the rapist monster. Thanks to the newly found journalistic trend of regional focus, newspapers were paying more attention to their immediate area of circulation; a monster killing people in Cape Town wouldn't be much news to people living in Johannesburg – or so thought the publishers.

Sizwe suddenly remembered that Kokoroshe had at some stage been studying in Cape Town. There was a possibility that he was still there. He phoned Kokoroshe's mother in Durban. She was ecstatic to hear his voice. They spoke briefly about nothing in particular. Then he asked her if she still had her son's number.

'Aw,' she said, 'don't you know what happened to him?'

'No,' he said, bracing himself for the worst, 'what happened?'

'He got a scholarship to go and study in Canada. He left six months ago already. Don't tell me you boys haven't been talking to each other since you left Durban?'

'Ah, yes, sorry. He did tell me he was leaving,' Sizwe lied, 'but I thought that was happening only next year.'

'No. He's gone already.' She gave him Kokoroshe's number in Toronto.

They said their goodbyes.

Sizwe made himself another cup of coffee, sat down at his desk, switched his computer on. He sipped his coffee slowly while waiting for the machine to boot up. Then he started writing.

Dear Brother,
I am emotionally drained, and mentally pulverised by what I've just seen in the paper. The story about your trial, your crimes. It boggles the mind how a person like you, on the surface so evidently normal, outgoing, cheerful, civilised, intelligent, imaginative, spiritually sound, can be found guilty of 153 charges of rape, kidnapping and indecent assault.

Far be it from me to delve into the details of your sordid crimes. The details are gory beyond mention, as you know. All I want to do is to express a cry from the depth of my heart, an anguished holler.

Brother, all these years I thought I knew you, but seemingly I didn't. My memory of you goes back to the first day we bumped into each other in the street. Remember? When you greeted me gruffly, trying to drive the fear of God into my heart. When I stood my ground you backtracked a bit, but then came back to spit in my face, and then later gave me the paraffin treatment. You were such a performer; have always been a performer, an attention-seeking piece of shit. I am joking of course. It is the likes of us who felt dwarfed by your presence, even if you didn't say a word or raise a hand. People listened to you, gravitated towards you.

Which is why I don't understand what you've just done. It doesn't make sense at all. You have all the power in your hands – intellectually and otherwise – you don't have to prove your power by raping people, by hurting them.

Remember how all the girls at school always swooned for you? Remember how you could bullshit teachers even when you didn't know the real, accurate answer, how you stretched your 'common sense' thing to the limit?

And the sermons you gave at your father's church, how your congregation hung on to every word you said? What happened to all of that? To that pride, self-confidence, visionary way of looking at things? I ask you what happened, dammit.

And then when you quit school, left your mother behind, you bestowed upon me so much of your work. I never realised you had written so much. And it's not just crap, it's powerful stuff. People are still raving about that 'Ramu the Hermit'. In fact they want me to send everything by Vusi Mntungwa. They want to do a collection of the shit – stories, poems, sketches, the lot. With all that talent – and literary talent is power, broer – you still felt inferior enough, powerless enough to want to impose your will upon defenceless women. And we're not talking about one, not two, not three but fucking more than a hundred women. Where would you have stopped had they not caught you? Answer me that, dammit!

Although you've refused to communicate with me, with your mom, with your past, I always knew you were alive somewhere. And then I see your face in the papers. And they are calling you Freedom Cele. Freedom Cele my ass! This Thulani Tembe, I scream out in anger as I look at your face in the newspapers. And when I tell my friends I know you, when I tell them just a bit of your story, they look at me, they look at each other, and I can see they don't want to believe me. Why did you change your name? Anyway I look at your face and they say you've raped all these people, I say fuckall, my friend is not capable of that, it must be some mix-up with the pictures. But then the story continues and I continue seeing your face alongside this Freedom Cele name and I say fuckit maybe I've gone crazy. I stop reading the papers. And later I hear you've been sentenced and I say fuck I must see this man.

But then I say, no, let me respect the man's wish. His last wish, before he turned his back on his family, his friends, his neighbourhood, was that he doesn't want to be found, doesn't want to be followed. Why, I even remember a letter threatening that you would kill us if we tried to find you. Anyway, I read the story about your sentencing and I say, fuck this brother of mine that I thought I knew I never really knew, and the brother I hadn't known must have been the real one.

My mind is suddenly filled with a contagion of emotions: sadness, horror, regret, a sense of betrayal, disgust. Please, brother, take me into the sanctum of your mind. What happened? I have been working my ass off here, selling the stories you wrote under that Vusi fucking Mntungwa name and all you do to thank me for the effort is rape and traumatise people. Fuck this, man!

You know that I as a writer, no matter how small my talent is compared to yours, have spent a respectable amount of my time immersed in the world of fiction – as a reader and writer. As a writer of fiction, I now realise that no matter how outlandish, how unimaginable my fictional stories might be, they fail to match what guys like you in the real world are doing to other people. What has happened to us human beings, broer? Tell me! I have never in my life had the opportunity to ask this question of a person so very well known to me. I have always thought that these monstrous things were a realm where strangers lived and operated. I never thought one day I would have a brother of mine having to respond to this kind of question.

I am sure you must have seen some of your stories published in various journals. People love them. When I tell them that the person who wrote them decided to disappear from the surface of the earth, they don't believe me. They think I wrote the stories, that I am trying to play some literary game. Maybe you should come out and reclaim what's yours. It makes me feel guilty every time I have to send one of your beautiful stories, I feel like a thief. In fact, to tell you the truth, I still wish God had given the talent that you have to a level-headed person like myself. I just don't want to understand your reasoning. Really, brother, you need to take me into the sanctum of your mind. Now that you're not in front of me, let me be bold once and for all and ask you this question: Did you steal the stories or not. If you did, who was the original author?

By the way, your mother doesn't realise that you are in there. Nor does anyone from the neighbourhood. It seems to me your picture only appeared in the Cape papers. Maybe that's the way you want it. Anyway, should I tell your mom and everybody else about your new identity, and where you are to be found?

Hahaha! So much for your attempt at disappearing from the face of the earth. You remember that Bob Marley song we used to sing as kids? You running and you running and you running away, but you can't run away from yourself. Must have done something that you don't want nobody to know about it.

But, broe, knowing that I am dealing with you, I do not necessarily expect a reply to this short missive. As you always reminded me, Bob Marley was a true prophet. I just wanted to vent my spleen so that you know how I feel.

Your brother Sizwe.

Then he remembered hearing that some jails set a 500-word-limit on mail to inmates. He set about editing the initial draft.

Twenty-Nine
Sales Pitch

By the time Sizwe arrived at the publishing house, his head was bursting with ideas.

'Heita, broe!' he greeted the security guard cheerfully. He explained that he had an appointment with Patrick McGuinness and Sheree le Roux.

The guard looked happy to see him. 'You know, broe,' said the guard, 'I love your newspaper columns. I've been longing to meet you and share a story or two with you.'

'I'm glad somebody even bothers to read the doggerel I write.'

'Truly, you are one of my joys. Can you imagine how boring a security guard's job can be! Anyway, from what you've written before – all those tirades against the Stalinists in our current government – I have a suspicion you will not be offended by the short story I'm going to relate to you.'

'Go ahead,' he said, masking the irritation that was getting the better of him.'

'Lenin was due to visit Poland. So, in recognition of the visit, the senior party people in Poland decided to commission a highly respected artist in one respected town to draw a picture on the theme "Lenin in Poland". They gave the artist two weeks to finish the work. However, just to be on the safe side, three days before the deadline, the local leader of the party, accompanied by some of his confidants, paid the artist a visit. The artist steadfastly refused to show them the work. He told them to come back the following day, by which time he would have completed it. Like the good communists they were, they didn't want to interfere with his artistic freedom, so they let him be, and went home. Next day, they stormed into the esteemed artist's studio and demanded to see the completed picture. The party leader spotted an easel in a corner. It was covered in a white sheet, which he ripped open. He suddenly felt dizzy when the image on the canvas sank into his consciousness. The picture showed Trotsky and Lenin's wife naked, getting into bed.'

At this both the security guard and Sizwe burst out laughing. The former regained his composure, and said: 'And so the party leader wanted to know from the artist: "But where is Comrade Lenin, you fool?" To which the artist answered very calmly, "But comrade leader, Comrade Lenin is in Poland."'

Sizwe was still wiping away tears of mirth as he walked off and found an elevator which took him to the second floor. Once there, he followed the directions he had been given, until he arrived at a reception desk.

He stated his business to a stern-looking woman seated behind a computer. She walked him to the boardroom where Patrick and Sheree were already waiting for him.

'Just in time for a warm lunch!' the woman whom he assumed to be Sheree beamed at him, extending her hand to be shaken. 'Good to meet you at last, please sit down.'

'It's always a pleasure to meet the people who make things happen in the literary world,' Sizwe said, trying to be cheerful. As a journalist, he had interacted with newspaper and magazine editors almost every day. But he had never met a real-life book editor before. He didn't know what he had expected a member of this species to look like, but Sheree's demeanour surprised him nevertheless. She was neither short nor tall, slim but not so thin as to be skinny. Her complexion was pale, indicating that she spent a lot of time indoors. Her hair was black and long. She wore a short-sleeved floral shirt, with the two top buttons open, showing a sexy bra which was almost the same colour as her skin. She wore an extremely tiny black skirt and tall black stilettos.

'Are you going to stand there gawking at my legs or are you going to sit down?' she said, laughing out loud like the seasoned women journalists he was familiar with. 'A lot of men who know that I am a dyke are always amazed at the way I dress. Hahaha! They expect us to dress like men, as many people expect moffies to dress and behave like women, with all those spaghetti wrists and feminine intonations: Ooooh, you look gorgeous, doll!'

'Ooooh, you look gorgeous doll,' Sizwe mimicked, and added, 'but where is Comrade Lenin? Hahahaha!'

'Oh, I see,' said Sheree cheerfully. 'Our lovely Joseph downstairs has introduced himself to you!'

They helped themselves to three takeaway packages of meat lasagne and cans of Coke. Then they started talking business.

'I definitely love "The Oneness", and would like to publish it alongside a collection of stories under your name. It will be a coup for the publishing house. But we have to move fast. Next year the country is having the first democratic elections. A historic moment. It would be crucial for us to climb the wave of goodwill and publish this very unusual text, as the first kind of book to herald a new society, a new South Africa. Ten months in publishing is nothing. We have to move fast.'

'I don't know if this is going to burst your bubble. But let me say it anyway. Thulani Tembe doesn't actually exist. The novel and the stories under the Vusi Mntungwa name are actually the product of my imagination, I wrote them.'

First there was alarm in Sheree's eyes, but she broke into a broad smile and turned to Patrick: 'So you were right all along. Brilliant! This is not a catastrophe but a great marketing opportunity. This is how I propose we move forward. We will release the works under the two different names. The writing styles are definitely different and the two names need to be marketed separately.'

'And I have a further suggestion,' said Patrick. 'I think a month or two before publication we run a series of articles introducing this writer Vusi Mntungwa and his work.'

'But he doesn't exist!'

'He does exist, it's just that he is a recluse. There won't be a picture of him.'

'But the market will find out sooner or later that Vusi Mntungwa is bogus, a hoax.'

'Then Vusi Mntungwa will come out of hiding, in the person of Sizwe Dube. The objective now is for Sizwe Dube, the highly respected literary critic, to write a series of in-depth profile pieces introducing this new writer Vusi Mntungwa. Once Vusi Mntungwa has gained currency as the hottest new writer to come in recent times, it will always be safe to reveal his real identity – Sizwe Dube. Or am I confusing you now. Maybe *I* am confused…'

'I don't know.'

'Use your contacts in the publishing world to give us space to write profiles on Vusi Mntungwa,' said Sizwe. 'The pieces will be based on what I remember about him and his first attempts at writing, a bit about the germination of "The Oneness".'

On that positive note, they finished the rest of the lunch and parted ways. He looked them straight in the eye, as befitted a good colleague, and licked his lips as if in anticipation of the task ahead.

Thirty
Letter from Behind Bars

Towards the end of 1993 a series of articles under the byline Sizwe Dube were published in the book sections of highbrow newspapers and magazines. The first article was more about the genesis of the book *The Oneness of Two in Three* than about the author. It did, however, hint at the fact that he was a recluse, one of the hottest new writers to emerge in the country.

The other articles were general think pieces about the state of South Africa. Basically, they were scene-setters pointing out that the South African literary landscape had not remained untouched by the major political upheavals that had characterised the country. A major literary phase was expected to accompany the political changes that would take place when citizens of all colours would, for the first time in the history of South Africa, go to the polls for the elections slated for April 27, 1994.

These articles were immediately followed by the publication of Sizwe's own collection of short stories entitled *A Temporary Inconvenience*. When the big novel itself, *The Oneness of Two in Three*, finally appeared in March, the literary pundits took to it with alacrity, calling it the definitive book for the new era, the voice of a new South Africa.

It was while the book was still the talk of the town that Sizwe received a letter with the Cape Town postmark. He knew immediately who it was from.

Dear Brother,
My initial instinct after reading the letter from you was to express remorse, to say how sorry I am at what I did. But then I realised I

had nothing to apologise for. He must apologise, the other guy must apologise. But he doesn't want to apologise. He's a stubborn, hard-headed piece of shit. I've been asking him to bare his soul, to pray to God for his sins, but he refuses. You don't follow me, do you? You see, there are three of us in me. No, I'm not schizophrenic. That's a shallow way of looking at the essence of being. What I am saying is that there are three of us in me.

First, there's the boy you know, the boy you grew up with. Then there is the other guy, Vusi Mntungwa, who is trying to be a writer. He is more dominant than the boy you know. Vusi is the guy who forced the boy to walk out of school. You see, Thulani is too much of a thinker, lives too much inside his head, thinks the world and humanity owe him a living. But he is not strong enough to want to fight for that living. He wants it on a platter. But the world doesn't operate like that. You have to fight to live. Simple as that. Every time Thulani tried to write something, to express his thoughts, Vusi would suddenly take over, the dominant bastard. Vusi has got a lot of things to say which clash with Thulani's moral code. Thulani is trying very hard to be a good human being, a good citizen, but he is too fragile to belong to the human race.

After Thulani and Vusi, there's Freedom Cele. He is the guy who got us here in prison. Freedom Cele is the devil-may-care who wants to fight fire with fire; the world is so cruel he wants to be more cruel than the world. Perhaps our being locked inside here is a blessing in disguise. There is no knowing what other sins Freedom Cele would have committed were we not inside. The three of us want our individual space.

It is a pity not a lot of people will understand what this is all about. But I hope, in fact I know, you will. You have the intellectual capacity to understand, the emotional depth to appreciate the design, such as it is.

It's such a pity I cannot throw much light on the subject of Freedom Cele's sins. He's such an asshole it's difficult to get inside his head. I am happy no one but you realises where I am, and I can only hope it remains that way. I want to be left alone. I trust you to keep it that way. My only consolation is that with this body behind the bars, no matter how pig-headed Freedom Cele wants to be, he can't do anything. This place is safe for us, it's good for our wellbeing.

But moving on to the little matter of those manuscripts, I am happy you respect my wish to use Vusi's name. Those are Vusi's stories. Thulani was bludgeoned into submission by this other asshole.

I have not seen the book itself, but I have been reading the rave reviews in the press. I like the way you have been consistent in telling the literary life of Vusi Mntungwa; I don't know if he agrees with the way you describe and view him. But let's hope you remain consistent in your perception and the picture you draw of him and his literary outlook. You have made him so much alive that it would be dangerous to kill him, or to alter him in any way.

Maybe I will get to see the book itself and look at how they edited it, maybe not. You see, I personally have no interest in writing now. Writing is a dangerous game to play, I must warn you. When I started, I was merely opening an avenue into my inner being, trying to open a conversation with myself, a dialogue with the many selves in me. But something went wrong on the way to self-discovery. Vusi came into his own, so did Freedom. So began the duel between them. And, as some of our African tribes say, when two elephants fight, it's the grass that gets hurt. That, in a nutshell, is the fate of Thulani. He's been trampled by the other two egoists. Too much self-knowledge is dangerous, I've since discovered.

Now, before I bid you farewell, let me remind you not to come visiting. Don't write to me again. If you do happen to write, don't say anything to me about the world outside. Good luck with your career.

Me.

Thirty-One
The Biography

Sizwe was kept busy over the next few weeks, giving interviews to TV and radio stations about his own collection of short stories, but, most importantly, sharing his expert knowledge with the public about this mysterious reclusive new writer, Vusi Mntungwa. There were, of course, nudge-nudge, wink-wink reviews and articles in some newspapers that insinuated that Mntungwa was, in fact, the alter ego of the one and only Sizwe Dube.

These articles suddenly gave Sheree from the publishing house an idea. She phoned Sizwe one day, her voice excited and panicky. 'Sizwe, I'm afraid we've lit a fire we can't control. Bookshops want more from Vusi Mntungwa, another novel, another collection of stories – anything, anything.'

'I've given you all I have. You've got that stack of stories and sketches and the other unfinished novel. But I think it's too jagged at the edges. It will be an anticlimax after the astounding success of "The Oneness."'

'Listen, I know you'll say I'm crazy, but what about this idea? Let's do a really postmodern thing. Let's look at doing a whole biography of Vusi Mntungwa. The suits upstairs, they have these permanent grins plastered on their faces. They just lurv Vusi Mntungwa. They would die to meet him. But of course you and I know he doesn't exist. So I've sold them the biography idea and they adore it. Think about it and come back immediately. Time is not on our side.'

Whenever he had to make a huge decision, Sizwe always liked going to his favourite restaurant in Randburg. It was on the second floor of a building located on the crest of a ridge. Stand on the balcony of the restaurant, and you have a panoramic view of Johannesburg and its suburbs. You feel like a king. You feel as powerful as if at the touch of a button you can transform the face of Johannesburg, indeed the face of the earth.

To the east, you can see as far as the airport, planes landing and taking off; to the south is the legendary Brixton tower and the famous Ponte City tower with its Coca-Cola neon sign, and beyond you have stretches of green trees. It's an amazing sight.

At night, the view is even more alluring, with Johannesburg spread out in front of you like a black gargantuan monster spread out at your feet, with countless blinking eyes, waiting for you to bark a command.

Whenever Sizwe stood there and appreciated the beauty and apparent wealth of the city, he could see exactly why it had taken so long for the whites to decide grudgingly to share political power and wealth with the black populace.

Writing a biography of Vusi Mntungwa would prove a nasty undertaking. If he based the Vusi Mntungwa biography on his own life, Thulani might come out of hiding and embarrass him, forever killing his credibility. On the other hand, if he decided to write the biography based on Thulani's life, those who knew Sizwe and his background might point out the incongruency between what he had written and the truth they knew about his life and work. He decided to err on the dangerous side: to write a biography that combined the personalities and histories of himself and his friend Thulani. After all, he had always felt almost the same as Thulani, or rather, had always wanted to be Thulani in some way.

Sizwe took solace in the fact that, no matter how angry Thulani might be, he might be mollified by the combination of their life stories. There was also an inkling of arrogance growing inside him, saying he shouldn't be too worried about a man who was behind bars, serving a long sentence. In fact he couldn't imagine his friend ever walking out of that prison. Even if Thulani got angry and complained, or wrote letters to the newspapers, no one would listen to him. A man convicted for more than a hundred instances of rape was sure to have a marble missing in his head. Who would believe such a man?

Fortified with this notion and two bottles of Chardonnay, he approached the restaurant manager and asked to use the house phone.

It was nine fifteen p.m. exactly when he dialled Sheree's home number: 'Sheree, I'll do the book, the biography.'

When he got home, he reached for the music system, fed in a CD, and pushed the play button. The room was enveloped in song:

> Come with me down Paradise Road
> This way please, I'll carry your load
> This you won't believe
> Come with me to paradise skies
> Look outside, and open your eyes
> This you must believe
> There are better days before us.

Over and over again, he played the song, sipping an umpteenth glass of wine, until tears started streaming down his cheeks.

Patrick, who had been busy in the kitchen, stormed into the lounge, shouting: 'Enough! Enough already! What's this syrupy shit you're playing, man? Who are these 'Paradise Road' chicks anyway?'

Roughly he pushed the stop button, plunging the room into a profound silence.

Sizwe continued humming 'Paradise Road', rocking back and forth. Finally, he said, still sobbing: 'I'm going to write the book, doll. I'm going to write the fucking biography no matter what he says, no matter what they say. I am going to fucking write the bloody thing, publish it and be damned!'

Thirty-Two
Thus Spake the Masses

The South African elections of 1994 were one of the biggest stories of the century. They marked the end of apartheid, the most abominable system of racial oppression in the world. They also marked the return of the country to the fold of the international community after more than three decades of isolation as a result of its segregationist, violent regime.

But to Sizwe this moment was just a blur he never got to appreciate, engrossed as he was in the biography, hardly sleeping and hardly venturing out of the house. He read few newspapers these days, relying on Patrick to keep the clippings that would be of interest to him. He was quarantined in his writing studio, with Patrick coming in now and then to give him food and drink. He also prepared a huge collection of zols, which Sizwe smoked one after the other as he wrote feverishly.

The room he wrote in was dark. There were letters strewn all over the place, newspaper clippings he had culled from Thulani's box of documents, typed manuscript from the same box, other boxes opened at strategic places or lying face down on the floor. The room smelt sweaty and male.

On the two occasions Patrick had been away for one-week stretches on some research project out of town, he'd come back to a smelly house. Now again, when he walked into Sizwe's den he realised what had happened: Sizwe had not bothered to get up and clean the plates he had been eating from. They lay in a pile in a corner. There were two Jack Daniel's bottles, both empty. The room even smelled of urine; when Patrick investigated, he found that Sizwe had urinated into one of the Jack Daniel's empties. He immediately ordered Sizwe out of the room, starting to clean even as he spoke. Sizwe, who was smoking a joint as he typed, smoke curling to his eyes, tried to resist: 'Look, I must finish this thing. He is coming to get me. He's out there.'

'Who?'

Sizwe looked around with wild, spaced-out eyes, put a finger across his lips, 'Shush! I can hear him coming. He mustn't hear us.' He'd put a trembling finger to his lips.

Patrick threw his head back and laughed, 'This is some good dagga, I told you so. Durban Poison.'

'How do you know he is from Durban? I never told you anything about him. But you already know he is from Durban? He is bringing the poison to kill me. He *is* the poison that will kill me.'

'Out now! Out!' Patrick dragged him out of the room, and opened the windows and started cleaning.

This was the first time in a long stretch that Sizwe had left the room. Suddenly he was sitting at another table having coffee and taking a quick glance at a newspaper that was eight days old. He was raring to get back to his writing table.

The paper was dominated by breathless stories about the election – what it meant for the economy, what it meant for the sporting world, and so on. Then at the bottom of page three was a tiny piece saying that the new president had announced that he would be extending a presidential pardon to five hundred prisoners – including the rapist Freedom Cele. On an ordinary day, this would have been the lead story. But in this edition it was choking under the froth of euphoric stories about what a bright future lay ahead for the country. Maybe the story had been given some prominence in the Cape papers, but the paper that Sizwe had in his hands was the local morning title.

Sizwe gasped in shock and disbelief, standing up from the chair with such speed that he spilt his coffee. He dialled the Cape Town prison.

***

Meanwhile, for Thulani, the elections were a traumatic period. In terms of some obscure constitutional provision, the new president was obliged to declare a presidential pardon to an X number of prisoners immediately after his inauguration, which took place on May 10, 1994. The names of those to be released were chosen at random. Thulani, as Freedom Cele, happened to be on the list, and had to go home. He was distraught.

He shared his terror with Hendrik Labuschagne, a man he had befriended inside. Hendrik had been a soldier just before he branched out into bank robbery. It was this new-found profession of his that had landed him in jail. After all the many talks he'd had with Freedom Cele the serial rapist, he still couldn't get over the fact that, of all the 105 – known – women he had raped, he had not killed a single one. He approached the women with a knife all right, threatened to use it on them, but once they co-operated he would put the weapon away and rape them.

'But what drove you to rape? I've heard it said that rape is a crime of power, a rapist is a fucking asshole with a low self-esteem who tries to compensate by turning his rage on powerless members of society,' Hendrik had said.

'No,' Freedom had responded, 'that's all intellectual bullshit. What Freedom has is an unencumbered personality – he takes a woman the minute he gets an urge. I've read in many magazines that men think of sex not less than twice in one minute – but the problem is that this suppresses the urge. Not Freedom Cele. The minute he thinks of sex, he goes out to get it.'

'Just like that?'

'Yep! Just like that. He's intention is not to hurt, not to dominate, but to satisfy the urge. Fullstop.'

That was sometime ago as they were sizing each other up, getting to understand each other. They had quite a few things in common, in that they were avid readers who frequented the prison library. They were also particular about their appearance – they went to the gym regularly and always came out tops in cleanliness. Their bunks were always immaculately made, their prison clothing spotless.

But now they were about leave prison, about to part ways.

'You're the weirdest guy I've ever seen,' Hendrik said now. 'Everyone of us here can't wait to get out of this fucking place and you are crying tears to be kept inside. You even talk about yourself as if you're someone else.'

'I have nowhere to go to. I have nothing to go back to. I am quite happy as it is here.'

'Come on, you're just a lazy bugger who's afraid to stare life in the face.'

'What is life?'

Hendrik rolled his eyes, groaned. 'Enough of this shit. When we leave in two days' time, you are welcome to stay with me. My brother-in-law has a nice big farm in the Eastern Transvaal, you can stay with us while you try to figure things out. You can work on the farm, you can join his security firm, the opportunities are limitless out there. His security firm has outlets all over the country, and they are contracted to most banks and shops. There's no way you can't find a job with him if you're telling the truth about having been a sharpshooter in your past. As for me, I can't wait to have some pussy. As for you, I think you've had enough pussy to last you a lifetime. Hahaha.'

Thulani was still not happy. He protested to the prison authorities, saying he didn't want to go home. That he had nothing and nowhere to go to. Unfortunately the officers couldn't defy the orders of those above them. So it was that Thulani was released with the others on June 16, 1994.

***

When Sizwe phoned after reading the paper, he was told the prisoners had been released ten days before. The officials at the prison could not give a forwarding address for Freedom Cele as he had left none.

***

It was in the middle of summer when Hendrik Labuschagne and his friend Freedom Cele arrived at the farm of Hendrik's brother-in-law, Piet Louw. As arranged, Piet fetched them from the Nelspruit bus terminus.

'You look quite well-fed for a couple of ex-cons,' Piet beamed at them.

'In Zulu we say: No one knows what made Mr Pig so fat,' Freedom said easily. Off the bat, he found this Piet Louw an affable, easygoing character he could banter with.

'So you ate every piece of shit that came your way, I suppose?'

'Even licked the plates clean and cried out for more.'

'You throats must be parched,' Piet said, ducking into the boot of his four-wheel-drive bakkie and coming back with six cans of chilled Castle beer. 'Have some.'

He gave them a can each, helped them dump their bags into the back, and they got into the car and drove off.

The verdant stretches of farmland – resplendent with sunflowers and groves of oranges – lifted the spirits of the two ex-cons, who hadn't seen much of Mother Nature's miracles in a long time. There were children peddling bananas, mangoes and other fruit by the roadside. They veered off the main road and took the Hazy View turnoff, heading north-east. This was banana land. Occasionally, they passed signs advertising the sweetest pancakes on earth.

About twenty minutes later they veered east, abandoning the tarred road, and were soon rattling on a narrow strip of gravel road.

'That's the farm down there,' Hendrik said, gesturing with his forehead at the valley below. His hands were busy feeding aromatic Rum Maple tobacco into the bowl of his pipe. They were still at the top of the slope, the road snaking steadily from the craggy face of the mountain down to a bowl of fertile land. The valley was secluded, as if a privately designed amphitheatre, walled in by mountains on all four sides, the only entry into the farm being the tiny road they were on.

'My brother-in-law is a real soldier, Freedom, look at his farm. It's like a fortress walled in by these huge mountains.'

'Quite a picturesque setup,' Freedom said, gulping down his second can of beer. 'But I never realised Piet was also a soldier like yourself.'

'Oh, yes, I did my service for my nation,' Piet said, taking a swig from his can of beer, 'except that I was on the other side, I was fighting on the side of the ANC against my swaer here.'

'Freedom tells me he was with the ANC, with what he calls the self-defence units. He's tried to explain to me what the SDUs were but I can't really say I understand.'

'Ag,' said Piet, 'it's simple. The SDUs were like your commandos.'

'Oh, easy as that? This darkie should have said so, I would have understood. They like complicating things, these darkies.' Hendrik winked at Freedom to let him know he was joking.

'But what were the commandos?'

'The commandos were like the SDUs, except the commandos' duty was to patrol white-owned farms and beat the hell out of any "suspicious" darkie they encountered along the way. Everybody happy with the definitions now?'

'Yes, comrade,' Freedom said. 'So you basically are the link between the old and the new order, the black and the white world?'

'You might say so.'

They disembarked from the car, and Piet helped them with their luggage.

'This is the main house, as you can see,' Hendrik addressed Freedom, 'and there are quite a few other outbuildings – servants' quarters, workshops where they fix things, stables for the horses and so on. But Piet will give you a tour of the farm once we've freshened up and settled in.'

They were ushered into a rambling room that looked like some kind of lounge. Freedom had seen this kind of house interior only in the movies. Scattered about were huge steel chairs covered with leather cushions so elaborately designed they could have been stolen from a museum. The wooden floor was covered with huge zebra skins. There were stuffed animal heads mounted on the walls: an impala, a zebra, a lion, some antelope, a cheetah. One wall was dominated by three flags: the flag of the old Republic of South Africa, the Vierkleur; the new Rainbow Nation flag, the well-known Y-front; and the black, green and gold flag of the African National Congress. Next to these, over a huge fireplace, were two crossed muskets. The room reeked of testosterone: sweat, cigars, stale beer.

Piet invited them to settle down. He disappeared into an adjoining room, coming back with a middle-aged man with a pronounced limp.

'Comrade Jack,' he said to the man with limp, 'this here is my brother-in-law I've been telling you about, and the other chap is his friend Freedom, another comrade.'

'Gentlemen,' Jack beamed at the two guests, shaking their hands warmly. Then he turned on his heels, taking the two men's suitcases with him.

'I met Comrade Jack in Angola, during the great mutiny,' said Piet. 'He was one of the few comrades who survived the purge, albeit with serious injuries during the shootout between the mutineers and the movement's security guards. I was one of those dispatched from Zambia to go and sit on the commission of inquiry into the whole mutiny shit. After the mutiny I stayed on a bit in Angola. When the leadership was satisfied that the mutiny had been thoroughly put down, I was one of those sent to Zimbabwe to start preparing for the passage of comrades from all over the continent back into South Africa. Leadership had by then started talking to the Afrikaner government, and the boers were making some interesting noises about releasing Mandela and coming to a negotiated settlement about the future of the country.'

They spent the rest of the evening eating, drinking, speculating about what could happen for South Africa under a new government. Piet Louw shared his farm with a troop of workers, some of whom joined in the merrymaking. They were mechanics, cooks, gunsmiths (who helped fix the guns for his security firm), and some security guards who commuted daily to the town of Nelspruit, where they protected shops and banks under the aegis of Emblem Security, Piet Louw's nationwide security firm.

Over the next few weeks, Freedom was shown around the farm. He joined Piet at the shooting range when the guards came for training once a week. Freedom used this opportunity to polish his shooting skills, acquired during the infighting between various black organisations after 1990.

Each day there were hours dedicated to physical training. Freedom revelled in Piet's fully equipped gym. His body had been moulded into a muscle-bunching fighting machine, thanks to the endless hours at the gym inside prison, but the equipment on the farm was even better. Sparring with the likes of Hendrik and Piet, both of them trained fighters, helped perfect his punching prowess.

Because Hendrik had told Piet everything about Freedom's past – at least the bits he was privy to – the farm owner decided not to send the new arrival out to work as a guard; instead, he put him in charge of his communications apparatus: writing press releases and dispatching these to relevant publications, answering calls to the company headquarters, making sure clients were properly billed and paid on time.

Piet Louw was overjoyed at the efficiency of this new friend. He was doubly happy because now he could stay away from the farm for days on end, secure in the knowledge that his clients were being seen to regularly and professionally. He had himself looked at marketing manuals written and designed by this new guy. Freedom's arrival suddenly freed Piet to visit clients more often, and go beyond South Africa's borders in search of new business.

More and more mining establishments and governments in Angola, the Democratic Republic of Congo and further afield were insisting on South African-trained men to protect their mines from rebels.

Piet Louw was also happy that the guy wasn't just a sissy confined to the switchboard. He could shoot, he had boxed with him and found him competent in hand-to-hand combat; he could come in handy in many scenarios.

And Freedom loved the job because it gave him a lot of time for himself – to think, scheme, dream. He was happy to be a world away from his past. He laughed at the thought of Sizwe pulling his hair trying to wonder where to look for him. That's how he liked it. To be missing, to be missed.

Thirty-Three
Night Nurse

Sizwe had worked himself into a dark corner of frustration. Over the past few months it had become apparent to him that he couldn't write a credible biography of Vusi Mntungwa by marrying the personalities of Sizwe Dube and Thulani Tembe. The Vusi Mntungwa who resulted from merging these two personas was not the Vusi he had in mind when he said yes, he would write the biography. He wanted someone unpredictable; someone with a dark secret who would want to disappear off the face of the earth just as Thulani Tembe had done; someone who could be as irrational as Freedom Cele. A combination of all that, but also credible enough to the outsiders who had read and loved *The Oneness of Two in Three*.

He had made quite a bit of money from the novel, and had already taken an advance against the royalties for the yet-unwritten biography.

What he did next shocked Patrick. He applied to be admitted as an inmate at the prison where Freedom Cele had served his time. To the authorities, he said he was writing a book on the famous rapist, but to his lover he was less straightforward.

The authorities had never been confronted with such a request. Frantic phone calls and e-mails were exchanged between those in charge, until the Minister of Correctional Services acquiesced – but on one condition: the writer could interact with the inmates during the day, during exercise time, but had to be locked away in a solitary cell after hours, for safety.

It was while Sizwe was away that Patrick, randomly rummaging through his lover's papers, came across a cutting of the story about

Freedom Cele the serial rapist. Stapled together with this was a glossy picture of a young man who bore a striking resemblance to the man in the newspaper picture. With his heart thudding at this discovery, he realised that the images in his hands were of the same man. The one in the glossy picture was the friend Sizwe had told him about, his childhood friend Thulani Tembe, but the man in the newspaper cutting was Freedom Cele – yet they were the same man.

Then there was the letter from Freedom Cele, alluding to the writing. Now Patrick realised that Vusi Mntungwa did in fact exist – he was the man who went around calling himself Freedom Cele. And Freedom Cele had been released from jail not so long ago, and Sizwe was hallucinating about a man who was chasing him... But then again, he could not imagine that the rapist and the boy in the picture could be the writer Vusi Mntungwa.

Still, he reached for the telephone and dialled Sheree's number. It was all so confusing. Maybe Sizwe had fabricated the letter from Freedom Cele, in his dagga stupor. He slammed the phone down before it started ringing.

***

The stay in prison lasted only three weeks, but when Sizwe came out he felt confident he could credibly capture the atmosphere. He was relaxed, full of ideas. All he needed now was to settle down in a more comfortable environment, think, plan, then start writing.

'When I was young, if I made soup...'

When he got home, Patrick wasn't there. By the third day, he still hadn't returned. It didn't matter much. He wanted to be alone after all. But a week later, he could feel he wasn't alone. Freedom Cele, or Thulani, or Vusi Mntungwa, or whatever the demon chose to call itself, was now with him in the house.

He decided to go out, allow the summer sunshine to bathe his face, the breeze to caress his skin, the light to banish the demons from his mind, into the dark past where they belonged.

For a whole week, and then another and another, he walked the streets of Johannesburg, drinking in gloomy pubs from the morning until the pubs closed for the day, or until he was kicked out for his habit of shouting, 'Get away from me, away from me, I wrote the books, not you. This is my literary legacy, fuck you. Where have you been all these years? Just tell me that.'

Under his armpit he carried a sheaf of typing pads into which he scribbled furiously every now and then. There was always a bottle of Old Brown sherry in one of his coat pockets. He called it his Night Nurse because it helped him cope, fighting away the demons closing in on him.

Time after time Patrick had to go and hunt him down, get people to overpower him and bring him home. He would clean him, nurse his latest wounds – but a few days later Sizwe would have escaped back to the streets. Patrick himself was not much help sometimes, as he kept sliding in and out of his cocaine stupors.

Within a month, gossip columns in the new tabloid papers were awash with stories about the famous author's escapades, his rough encounters with barmen and bouncers. He walked around in rags, his mouth and ears suppurating with sores, his breath rank, his whole body a host to myriad parasites.

And then one day a letter came addressed to Sizwe. Patrick sat back and wondered where his lover would be right now, then quickly opened the letter and read it. The message was terse:

> I don't like what's happening to you. I feel so. I need to see you so we can exorcise the demons once and for all. Maybe it's time I took charge of the writing once again.
> Yours sincerely, Vusi Mntungwa

Thirty-Four
Flying High in Empty Sky

It had been Freedom Cele's intention to visit Sizwe Dube. He had been following his friend's literary successes with the vigilance of an eagle. Although the world of writing was now behind him, he'd been happy for his friend who was still obsessed with writing. Freedom Cele was ambivalent about revealing himself to Sizwe until he started reading stories about his friend's descent into madness and self-mutilation. Now the intention to visit became palpably urgent.

For his own part, he was excited that he, Freedom Cele, was being allowed by fate to take the path he had chosen for himself, the path of a soldier, a person who couldn't foretell his future. His job at Emblem kept him on edge, the life he enjoyed most. As a rapist he had lived on the edge, not knowing what the future held in store for him. The new job held the dark promise of suspense and excitement. He thrived on that. Could not have enough of it.

He was tempted to phone Sizwe's parents and alert them to their son's misery, for he suspected that as people who scarcely read newspapers, let alone stories about demented writers, they were not likely to be aware of their son's descent into madness.

But his dream of seeing Sizwe was not to be. Emblem Security had just landed a huge contract to protect the manganese mines of a senior government official in Zimbabwe. Freedom was therefore kept busy writing press releases on this major coup, and also helping his boss with the paperwork on service agreements and such.

Three weeks later he learnt that he would be travelling with his boss and about ten other Emblem men to help lay the foundations for this, their first major foreign deal.

Because there just had been an attempted coup in Kisangani, where they were to be stationed, they had to be well prepared for increased rebel incursions into the manganese-rich area near by. Being well prepared would mean well armed and alert. Ninety-two men were hand-picked by Piet Louw himself as the crack squad to go to the heart of darkness, the DRC.

It took them a whole week to revise and re-revise the maps of the terrain they would be patrolling. Apart from ninety-five R1 rifles and twenty RPG rocket launchers, the bulk of their weaponry would be collected from Zimbabwe, where they would stop over for a day or two.

Ever since the new president of South Africa came to power, the country had been going out of its way to play a leading role in the campaign to restore African pride, leading the African Renaissance – and part of that process was the long, arduous task of systematically disarming countries in the southern African region in order to reduce local conflict. When South Africa stopped supplying arms to neighbouring countries, rebel forces there turned to gunrunners operating mainly through Zimbabwe. It was a roaring trade with syndicates from all over the world.

Freedom Cele was not privy to all the intricacies of the gunrunning routes. All he was interested in was the promise of excitement ahead, real opportunities of being involved in active combat. Judging by what the newspapers were saying, a lot of blood was being shed where his group was going – and that's what he was looking forward to.

The bus ride from Nelspruit to Johannesburg was not comfortable; the bus was jam-packed with all ninety-two Emblem men destined for the DRC. They were relieved to disembark at Lanseria airport, where an aeroplane was already waiting for them. Airport staff helped them pack their equipment into the hold.

Their paperwork done, they boarded the plane for its first destination, Zimbabwe. It had a huge capacity, the better to accommodate the extra military hardware they would pick up from their contacts in Harare.

Freedom Cele, like many of the men, had never been aboard an aeroplane in his life. Sitting in his own comfortable seat now, sipping from a can of beer and chewing on strips of biltong, he felt like a king, floating in the deep blue skies, floating to the destiny of the unencumbered man that he was. But every now and then, he wondered what awaited him at the other end. Now and then his other persona, Thulani Tembe, would try to take over, asking questions about where Sizwe Dube was at the moment, how he was coping, but the dominant Freedom soon wrested control from the Thulani, putting himself at centre stage, cracking jokes with colleagues. What a simple, straight-talking guy, they told each other.

Thirty-Five
Killing Time

With Sizwe's descent into madness and booze, Patrick himself succumbed to the dark demons of the past. He started walking the streets again – this time becoming one of Daddy Cool's charges. The pimp was happy to have this white boy coming to his senses once more.

'No bitch can walk these mean streets of Jo'burg without Daddy Cool's say-so, you hear me, bitch?' the thug was saying, leaning against a cupboard in his huge kitchen. Patrick was on his knees, working his tongue round Daddy Cool's erect member. There were tears in Patrick's eyes as he thought of Sizwe, whom he was missing so immensely. Caught as he was in the throes of his own desperation, he had given up on trying to help the person who mattered most in his life.

'Everyone that I treasure dies,' Patrick was thinking, fears running down his cheeks. 'My parents are dead, now Sizwe is practically dead.'

'Bitch,' Daddy Cool was saying. 'Why are you crying down there? You love my dick so much you have to shower it with your tears? Suck as passionately as you want, just don't bite me! There's a huge reward waiting for you. I truly love this new South Africa and it's democracy. Who ever thought black Daddy Cool would have a white man's tongue wrapped around his black dick, whoa!'

Daddy Cool was measuring a packet of cocaine. While working down there in the nether regions of his boss's body, Patrick couldn't wait for a strong hit of cocaine to transport him to a world of bright lights, loud music, smiling faces; out of the misery of life without his Sizwe. Something to take him away from the misery of consciousness and pain.

On the other side of town, Sizwe was sitting belly up at the bar inside the crowded Rich Man Poor Man pub in Hillbrow. He was in one of his rare moods of lucidity, when his mind was clear and his mood indifferent. He was nursing a cold Castle draught, absent-mindedly watching TV with the sound turned off. There was a murmur of voices in the background, wisps of smoke rising to the ceiling, where a fan was whirling, recycling the smell of stale beer.

'When I was young, if I made soup...'

He loved it here because for one, the beer was cheap; secondly, everyone minded his own business, drinking, swearing and fighting with careless abandon. No one told you how to dress. Above all, the place stayed open from ten in the morning until two a.m.; at weekends it stayed open almost twenty-four hours – as long as there were still people standing, albeit staggering and vomiting all over, the barman wasn't allowed to shut up shop.

The pub also played some of the best jazz music around town. Right now, the speakers hidden somewhere in the ceiling were booming with the sound of Kippie Moeketsi and his band. Kippie was in full flight, playing 'Memories of You', with Abdullah Ibrahim on piano.

A story had once been told to Sizwe by one of his jazzophile friends how Kippie learnt to improvise. The tiny saxophonist had been trained classically, one of the first of his generation to read a music score. One night he was jamming with one of the big bands. All the senior players were taking long solos, boring Kippie almost to tears. Kippie, with about six bottles of beer in his belly and at least three zols of dagga in his head, suddenly decided it wouldn't hurt him at all if he could close his eyes just for a tiny weeny moment while awaiting his turn. So he obeyed his body and closed eyes while standing there amid other members of the brass section. He was on the threshold of dreamland when he felt a harsh voice shouting at him, 'Kippie. Solo!'

He opened his eyes, looking this way and that before realising what was happening, wiping a sling of saliva from the corner of his mouth. And he blew like a madman, delivering one of the best solos of his career.

Like Kippie waking up from his stupor, Sizwe was startled by what he was seeing on TV.

'Bra Tim,' he called out, drawing the attention of the barman. 'Can you put up the volume on TV just one tiny notch?'

'Fuck TV,' someone shouted, 'if the professor wants to watch TV he should have stayed home. We came here to drink and catch up with the real news, the news that affects us directly from the gentlemen's mouths, jy ken?'

The barman was decisive: he turned the TV volume up, and softened the music. Now everyone had their eyes glued to the screen. The newsreader was telling how ninety-two South African men had been arrested in Zimbabwe on suspicion that they were mercenaries on their way to stage a coup in the DRC. The men, already in their jail uniform, were being paraded for everyone to see. Sizwe recognised the Information Department building behind where the men were standing, with armed guards hovering near by. Sizwe had gone there a number of times on assignment.

Sizwe blinked repeatedly at the TV screen. He seemed to recognise one of the men as his old friend, Thulani Tembe, or Freedom Cele, or whoever he was these days. Or was he confused again?

A correspondent in the DRC was filing a report by phone, quoting impeccable sources as saying the South African men's accomplices in the DRC had already been captured and were to face the firing squad the following day. That was the minimum sentence for treason in that country; instant justice, no trial.

Sizwe gulped his beer in a hurry and left the pub, moving like a wraith in flight along the busy streets of Hillbrow.

Over the next two days, Sizwe worked feverishly on the background to the story. He discovered that the South African men had left South Africa on the understanding that they would have a stopover in Zimbabwe. Once there, they had their papers confirmed for passage to the DRC. In the meantime, the head of the team, one Piet Louw, had transferred money to the account of a senior official in the Zimbabwean defence force, who also happened to be a member of a semi-independent body that procured arms on behalf of the Zimbabwean government. The same agency, he noted, handled the distribution of arms from Zimbabwe to other countries in the region.

In the two days they spent in Zimbabwe, the men were entertained by senior government ministers and taken on sightseeing tours of the country. One of these was the Heroes Acre, where the men who fought for the independence of Zimbabwe lay buried. Just a few metres away was an open piece of ground where, the men were told, traitors to the state were normally killed by a firing squad. This area was called the Parade Grounds.

Departing from Zimbabwe, the South Africans were in a jovial mood as they walked towards their plane, which had been parked in a hangar normally reserved for the country's military aircraft. Their luggage and the hardware they had come to buy had already been loaded. They were dressed casually, some of them carrying cameras, and frolicked about before the last leg of the trip. When they were all on the tarmac, they were surprised by a swarm of armed soldiers who approached them with raised rifles. Someone used a loudhailer warning them to stand still with their hands in the air.

Some of them had smiled stupidly, thinking this was some kind of game. But it wasn't a game at all. They were under arrest on orders from the president, who had been contacted by his counterpart in the DRC.

In the first week, the speculation was that they would be extradited to the DRC, where they would experience Congolese justice. But then things changed. Zimbabwean officials had discovered that the men had flouted their arms control laws – in collusion with the head of the arms procurement agency, who had since fled the country.

Meanwhile, the South African government had washed its hands of the matter, saying the men had left South Africa illegally and therefore had to face the consequences of breaking the law in both countries.

In short, they were on their own. Sizwe decided to fly to Zimbabwe so he could be there on the day of their execution by firing squad. They were to be killed ten at a time.

First he called at the Central Prison in Harare, where the men were held. He was told that the men were not allowed to see anyone as they were on death row. Even his threats of reporting the prison officials to his friend the Minister of Information had no effect.

'In fact, comrade, we've killed eighty-two of them already,' an affable officer told him. 'We have ten more to go. You will have the pleasure of seeing them die tomorrow morning. Be there.'

'I'm particularly interested in one of them,' Sizwe said, reaching into his briefcase and fishing out a newspaper cutting with the picture of the convicts. He pointed out the face that had been circled in a red pen.

'Sorry, comrade,' the officers shook their heads, 'we don't know if he's in tomorrow's group or if he's been fed to the birds of prey already. What's so special about him, in any case?'

'Ag, never mind.' He turned on his heels and went back to his hired car.

For one who had spent the past few months in a state of derangement, he was surprisingly clear of mind as he freshened up in his hotel room, and steadily spread out on his bed hundreds of typed manuscript pages, sipping a beer. Later, he changed into fresh clothes and walked to the bar downstairs.

He was into his fourth beer when a man walked in quietly and sat two seats away from him. When he looked at Sizwe, their eyes locked. The man looked vaguely familiar. Where could he have seen him? Back home in South Africa? Or somewhere in the many watering holes he had visited before in Harare? He couldn't decide.

The man spoke: 'I don't like what you're doing.'

'What am I doing?'

'You are bothering me. You are tailing me, following me wherever I go.'

'What the hell are you talking about? I got here first and *you* are bothering *me*. If you aren't careful I'll have you thrown out. All the security guards around here know me.'

When Sizwe took a long swig from his drink, the man did likewise, then turned to him and said, 'I don't care if you know all the security guards in the world, you are still following me.'

'Following you? Who are you?'

'I should be asking you that question? Who do you think you are following? And who *are* you?'

'I am sitting here by myself, trying to have a quiet drink by myself, and...'

'You don't understand me,' the man said patiently. 'That's exactly what I mean. You are trying to be me. Trying to get into me.'

'Talking shit!' Sizwe shouted now. 'Talking shit!'

The barman started in his direction: 'Sir, what is the problem? Can I be of assistance to sir?'

'This motherfucker piece of shit. He is talking shit!' Sizwe said, waving his hand in the direction of the stranger.

The barman looked where Sizwe was pointing, and said, 'But, sir, there's no one here.'

Sizwe looked around, and said, 'But he was here!'

'Sir has been the only customer in the bar for the past hour, sir. Officially the bar is closed now, but seeing that sir is a regular customer, we can't chase sir away.'

'You talking shit! Patronising me! You are hiding the man who was bothering me just now! Management will get to know about this, I tell you.'

'When I was young, if I made soup...'

Thirty-Six
Men in Black

Next morning Sizwe did not have much of an appetite for the otherwise sumptuous breakfast that had been placed before him. He speared the crisp bacon with his fork and started slicing it with his knife. He suddenly felt sick of the very sight of the meat. He turned on the scrambled egg, scooping it with his fork and forcing it into his mouth. He swallowed with difficulty. In order not to spit it all out, he forced it down with a generous gulp of his orange juice. He stood up and walked towards the communal smorgasbord where there was a variety of fruit. He grabbed a banana, an apple and a small tub of yoghurt.

He walked out to his car, which the attendant had parked in front of the hotel. He got into his car and started driving mindlessly.

A block away from the hotel, he hit a roadblock.

'Good morning, sir,' one of the policemen said politely, 'you'll have to turn into this street here, because Rotten Row is closed off for the exclusive use of the presidential motorcade.'

'I take it the president is driving to the Parade Grounds then?'

'Yes, of course. Is it also your intention to go and witness the meting out of justice, sir?'

Sizwe nodded.

'You have to turn this way, and move very fast so that you are far ahead of the motorcade. Once the president has reached the grounds, entrance will be closed off to the public.'

He thanked them and drove like a bat out of hell.

In the public parking lot outside the grounds, he was shown to one of the last remaining bays by a uniformed guard.

'Run, comrade, they are about to close the gates to the public.

Comrade president is on his way.'

By the time he got inside, he was sweating hard. All the booze from the night before was coming out of his pores. Systematically he negotiated his way through the throng of people, everyone of them excited, craning a neck to get a better view of the ten men who were already standing on the raised platform, their hands tied behind their backs, members of the firing squad caressing their guns close by.

'Traitors! Traitors! Traitors!' the crowd was chanting, stomping the grounds, sending up ghosts of dust into the air.

The sun was oppressively hot now. Sizwe finally found himself a spot which gave him a good view of the condemned men. He surveyed them carefully, looking for the familiar face of his friend Thulani. With growing panic he realised that he wasn't among the men in front of him. He reached for the newspaper cutting, looked at the picture carefully, trying to match the face in the picture with one of the faces paraded in front of the enraged crowd.

It was with relief that he discovered that his man was there: Prisoner Number 2005. Gradually he eased through the crowd and stood almost alone in front, his eyes immediately meeting those of the prisoner. When he blinked he realised that the prisoner he'd thought was his friend was actually a very dark-skinned stranger with a face full of scars. Or was that right? It went on like that for quite a while, his eyes playing tricks with him.

The president and his entourage had finally been ushered onto a makeshift platform with a clear view of the proceedings – the soldiers getting ready with their guns.

Suddenly, Sizwe felt trapped in a world where only he and Prisoner 2005, his man, existed. They were facing each other, and the man spoke: 'Don't go looking for the living among the dead.'

'That was a reference to Jesus Christ,' Sizwe said. 'Except you've twisted the words somewhat.'

'The person you're looking for, he who is two in one, Vusi Mntungwa and Thulani Tembe, is dead.'

'But he can't be dead. Because I made him. I created him through my writing. I have to kill him. This is why I am here, to see that he is dead.'

'But you have failed. You never succeeded in creating him, because you could not even understand a part of him, you couldn't understand Thulani. That's why you've been stumbling on all these obstacles all your life. You were trying to understand Thulani. But he always beat you at whatever you tried.'

'Fuck off!'

'*You* fuck off.'

Now the crowd had joined Sizwe in the chant. 'Fuck off! Fuck off!'

When he looked at the man he thought was Thulani, he realised that he would never win. His eyes continued playing tricks with him.

Thirty-Seven

Murderous Thoughts, Murderous Words

Sizwe was walking on the dusty ground as if in a dream. Suddenly, there was a voice shouting from a distance, 'Hey, what are you doing here?' He looked around, but could not see anyone. He continued walking. He heard the sound of approaching footsteps. He stood still and waited. Out of the gathering darkness he saw a man in a security guard's uniform.

'It's time to go home now, comrade,' the man said in a friendly voice, 'no one is allowed to walk about these holy grounds after dark. Go home, comrade. Justice has been done. The dogs are dead and buried, comrade. We burnt the remains of their bodies and disposed of their ashes down the river. We can't waste burial ground. Law-abiding citizens of this country are dying; they deserve to be buried properly, with dignity, in real graves. Aids is prancing proudly about. We are running out of burial grounds. Dogs such as the ones we killed today can't be allowed to exacerbate the problem. They need to be disposed of like the dogs they are. Ha-ha-ha!'

Sizwe didn't respond, just kept on walking.

'I know what it's like, comrade. Some of us decent citizens are sometimes labouring under the misguided belief that dogs such as these should be kept in jail instead of being put before the firing squad. I know exactly what you're thinking. And I suspect this is the first time you've seen our firing squad in action. Efficient fellows, these, ha-ha-ha.' The guard paused. 'You are not a man of many words, are you, comrade?'

'Words are lethal. Words are dangerous. They betray us to the world in which we move. Once you open your mouth to utter a word, you've bared your soul to the world. You've exposed your essence, your spirit, to the world in which you move. Words are ideas. Aside. Dies A. A dies. They are molecules of one's soul. Piled on each other, one after the other, words formulate a body of thought, a body of belief.'

'What you're saying is that the dogs we killed today were killed by their own words, their ideas, their beliefs?'

'Precisely. Look at you. You've just used the word "dogs". That's what you believe. But look at that word again. It can also spell "gods". A radical departure from the way you are using it. Those people could be "gods", depending on the beholder's point of view, depending on what kind of gods. It's all a matter of orientation, of interpretation, of belief. Those people could have been killed for using the wrong words at the wrong time. Or for their inability to use words at all. Dogs. Gods. Words. Sword. Dogma. Ma god. Am god. Ma dog. Am god. Words. Sword. Ideas. Aside.'

They reached the gate to the shooting ground. Sizwe said goodbye. He got into his car. He headed for town.

The streets glittered with colour, with neon lights having come to life. Nightfall had bestowed upon the city a vibrancy which had not been there during the day. In flat daylight the city looked bleak, with its decaying buildings. The city, like most cities in the world, was like an old whore who, under layers of make-up and the glittering lights of the brothels and nightclubs, looked young, vivacious, alluring; come daytime, stripped of these embellishments, she looks haggard, sickly, forlorn.

Much later, in his hotel room, he found on his writing table a note that read:

Brother,
It has saddened my heart very much that you've spent a huge part of your life running after me. I seem to have eluded you right up to the point they put me in my grave. You never could catch

up with me. I never left town, I was always there by you, but in your desperation to be me you could not even recognise me in the street, so entrapped you were in your world of finding out who I really was. But I hope the journey has been worth the trouble. I hope it's not the end of the journey, keep walking, maybe you will finally find out who I really am, and who you really are.
Your brother,
Oneness of Two in Three

With the note still in his hands, he ran downstairs to the reception desk.

'Where is he?' he asked the receptionist breathlessly, 'where is the man who left this message?'

The receptionist craned his neck to have a better look at the scribbled note. Having read it, he smiled at Sizwe, saying, 'But sir, you wrote the message.'

'You shut up! Just shut the fuck up!' he shouted so loudly that people being served at the other end of the reception desk looked up in amazement. 'I couldn't have written this.'

'But sir, I was on duty last night. Before you proceeded to your room, you asked me to give you a notepad and a pen, which I gladly did. You wrote the message, and ordered that it be delivered to your room this morning, which the concierge did promptly at ten a.m. as you requested.'

'You all are fucking liars! You are hiding the man who has been stalking me!' He jumped over the counter and fell on the receptionist with his punches. Within minutes, hotel security managed to overpower him.

About an hour later, four men in black suits, white shirts, black ties and the ubiquitous dark sunglasses of the Central Intelligence Organisation sat in Sizwe's hotel room, methodically going through the typed pages from his briefcase.

A couple of these pages had the following words typed over and over: Running away from yourself, running away from yourself, running away from yourself...'

Then there was a copy of a novel entitled *The Oneness of Two in Three,* by Vusi Mntungwa. A huge head-and-shoulders picture had been stapled to the back cover. The face in the picture was unmistakably that of the man who had attacked the receptionist downstairs – Sizwe.

And then, among the many jumbled documents in the briefcase, the intelligence people found what looked like personality profiles of each of the ninety-two men who had been arrested as mercenaries said to be planning a coup against the DRC regime.

The agents were riveted. One of them said what they were all thinking: 'This Freedom Cele guy is one of those thugs in custody. He was supposed to have been one of those killed by the firing squad today, but the officers decided to spare him. He will only be killed later in the week, from what I've heard. The fool downstairs has to be linked to the suspected mercenaries. Let's take him to the station where we can interrogate him in the presence of his lookalike, Freedom Cele.'

'Comrade agent, bring all those profiles and fake writings with you. I suspect that novel is also fake. Who's ever heard of a novel with such a title? It's meant to confuse us, I guess.'

It was a sweltering day outside as the car with the four agents and their sedated prisoner sped down Rotten Row towards the headquarters of the CIO.

'Why is this fool keeping on shouting that Freedom Cele is dead?' said one agent.

'Who is this Freedom Cele? I think this guy is plain deranged.'

'You can never know about these South Africans, comrade. I used to think only the white ones were mad. I'm not so sure any more.'

'Problem with the black ones is that while we were fighting the white man, they were busy trying to sound like him, trying to be him; now they've been infected with all their white diseases including greed, madness, identity crises, all manner of shit. Ayi, ayi, ayi!'

The prisoner opened his eyes slowly. He looked around. He

realised that he had no chance in hell of fighting against the men in black. Or trying to get them to understand him. To appreciate that he was as lucid as they were. So, taking a leaf from the book of Nelson Mandela who saw good sense in a negotiated settlement for his country instead of an all-out war, he spoke slowly and clearly: 'Gentlemen of Zimbabwe, comrades who fought in the chimurenga, I have no fight against you. I realise that you are justifiably concerned, even paranoid, about the safety of your country. After all, the world is crawling with spies and terrorists, and one has to go the extra mile to protect the citizenry of one's country. I salute and respect you, comrades. You and our comrades from our liberation movements fought side by side against the colonialist oppressors at Wankie and in many other battles. All I am asking you is this: Do you realise what I have been through? I've been through hell and back. And shit!' He raised his eyebrows challengingly and said, 'Do you know what you're dealing with? Do you know who I am?'

'Well,' one agent said heartily, 'do you?'

'You know, officers, when I was young, if I made soup and was chopping the onions, I thought I was the onions, I thought my friend Thulani Tembe, also known as Freedom Cele, also known as the Oneness of Two in Three, was the knife. I thought he was the knife chopping me, the onions. He was the knife chopping me, making me feel small, making me feel untalented, making me feel like losing my identity in his.'

***

'Counsel, I suppose what I'm saying is…' The man let the words hang in the air. He got up steadily from his chair, brushed his shoulder-length hair away from his face, and took a handful of sadza, rolled it into a ball and dunked it into the bowl of chicken gravy. He ate noisily, letting gravy drip from the corners of his mouth. He scooped a handful of spinach and shovelled it in too.

It was Dries van Wyk Louw's mission to irritate the man sitting across from him at the table, Advocate Simba Chigumburi, the most senior officer within Zimbabwe's feared Central Intelligence Organisation.

'Counsel,' Simba countered patiently in his Ivy League accent, pecking with his knife and fork at the Greek salad, 'you have been in this country for two full weeks, but you have failed to prove to us why your client cannot be linked to the dogs of war that were put before the firing squad the other day. Here we have Sizwe found in possession of identity documents belonging to Thulani, one of the mercenaries. And you still say he is innocent.'

'Exactly my point, counsel, the man is crazy. He is beyond schizophrenia. He is afflicted with a condition I've never encountered before. He has internalised somebody else's identity.'

'Show us medical proof, sir.'

Dries, an advocate of long standing himself, now stood haughtily in front of his adversary, thinking, What the hell does this piece of shit think he is? He did not mind that his hands, dripping with gravy, were planted firmly on his hips, staining his khaki trousers. He was a clumsy man who had long ago made peace with his clumsiness. His face was covered by scruffy patches of beard; and his lanky hair, which kept coming into his face, looked in desperate need of a shampoo. But it was his eyes that unsettled Chigumburi. They were huge, bulging, uncomfortably too big for his head; yet in tone they were flat, as muddy as those of a crocodile.

For his part, Dries was studying this dainty snob of a darkie, groomed to the point of being irritating – what with his fresh Mike Tyson cut, his dainty little spectacles, his designer moustache, his sky-blue shirt with deep blue braces to complement it, pure gold cufflinks and a white diamond dress ring to round things off. And, oh, look at it, dainty little fingers with freshly manicured nails.

Yes, he certainly despised the mannerisms of his adversary. But he admired his education and intellect. Before coming here, Dries had studied his file and learnt that Chigumburi held a master's degree in commercial law from Yale; had taught law there; had been made junior partner at one of the most prestigious law firms on Wall Street – all of this before he turned thirty. Now he was among the most highly regarded lawyers in Zimbabwe, and was in charge of the CIO.

The two men had been circling each other for a number of days now, Dries trying to show why his client Sizwe had to be released from prison: he was not a threat to the safety of the state of Zimbabwe, because he was a mental patient. Chigumburi, on the other hand, had insisted that the Zimbabwean authorities had enough evidence to prove that a plot to oust the government of Zimbabwe was being hatched within the borders of South Africa, and Sizwe could not be ruled out as one of the co-conspirators.

'Counsel,' Dries started patiently again. He sat down and took a swig from his can of Coke. He burped loudly, brushing his stomach. 'I suppose you've had a look at the documents that were found in the possession of my client?'

'Yes, a pile of papers that make no sense at all. It's a modus operandi of these operatives to try and sow confusion wherever they go, to create mystery around the identities and their motives. You South Africans surely take us for fools.'

'Counsel, I'm not going to argue on matters of law, on matters of legal principle.'

'Yes, because you have no case.'

'You have to prove motive, you have to prove a link between my client and the mercenaries.'

'We already have a link. The link is a man called Freedom Cele, or Thulani Tembe.'

That stopped Dries. 'The name Freedom Cele wasn't mentioned among those mercenaries who were put before the firing squad.'

'It's because Freedom Cele is still alive. In custody. He is due to face the firing squad soon. I've been trying to piece together his identity from what he's been telling us. A lot of the things he says seem, somehow, to suggest that he thinks he is your client, or the man you call your client, the man you are trying to get out of this country.'

Dries got up quickly from his chair, almost toppling the table in his excitement.

'Counsel, please let me see this Freedom Cele. I would like to interview him.' Then he muttered to himself, 'I think something is coming together now. This Freedom Cele will possibly trigger something in my client's mind. And we can take it from there, try to track the families of both men. I'm saying this because my client keeps calling himself Freedom Cele, and he goes on about a part of him, a part of his identity that's gone missing.'

'Are you trying to tell me that the man you call your client has internalised the identity of Freedom Cele, the man we are going to put before the firing squad?'

'Counsel, I don't know what's going on. But I think the identities of the two men have been fused so much that the men themselves do not know who they are, or who they want to be.'

'Typical of South Africans,' the Zimbabwean advocate mumbled as he got up.

What he hadn't told Dries was that the release of his client was imminent. A handwriting expert had confirmed that the specimens found in Sizwe's possession – all of them, including those attributed to the various personas he had used – had been written by Sizwe. A psychiatrist who had been given access to Sizwe's writings and other personal items was waiting back in South Africa. He had found enough evidence that Sizwe thought he was more than one person. Preliminary detective work had uncovered stacks of photographs with the face of a man who seemed to be a younger version of Freedom Cele, the condemned man. It was now their job to find out why the man called Sizwe would so much want to be Freedom Cele. What was clear to all parties concerned, however, was that Freedom Cele was in fact Thulani Tembe, who had grown up with Sizwe Dube.

'What does Sizwe Dube stand to benefit by trying to be Freedom Cele?' Chigumburi grumbled to himself again. 'These South Africans are fucked up, always were.'

In his cell, in one moment of complete sanity, Sizwe Dube was chattering on: 'Clearly *I* can't be *him*. Only if they kill my friend Thulani, the man they call Freedom Cele, will I regain my own identity, my pride in myself. Why do I still think of him as my friend? He's stripped me of my self-respect, dignity and belief in myself. He must die.'

Other fiction titles by Jacana

Bitches Brew
by Fred Khumalo

A Bit of Difference
by Sefi Atta

Sunderland
by Ken Barris and Michael Cope

Unimportance
Hear Me Alone
by Thando Mgqolozana

The Unsaid
The Big Stick
Six Fang Marks and a Tetanus Shot
by Richard de Nooy

I See You
by Ishtiyaq Shukri

The Book of War
Walk
by James Whyle